"Would You Like To Get Something To Eat?"

Rance asked Darvi tentatively.

"I don't know...."

He saw the uncertainty come into her eyes. "For crying out loud, Red. I'm just talking about grabbing a bite. I'm not asking you to be the mother of my children." The words had come out of his mouth before he could stop them. Children were not a subject he cared to discuss, and certainly not with someone who had a very definite, albeit confusing, effect on his senses.

Her anger flared to match his outburst. "I told you not to call me Red! I don't want to have to tell you again." She glared at him. *The mother of my children* were the last words she wanted to hear from anyone, least of all Rance Coulter.

Dear Reader:

News flash!

The Branigans Are Back!

All of you who have written over the years to say how much you love Leslie Davis Guccione's BRANIGAN BROTHERS will be thrilled and pleased that this rambunctious family is back with *Branigan's Break*.

More Fun from Lass Small!

We start the New Year with a fun-filled *Man of the Month* from one of your favorite writers. Don't miss *A Nuisance*, which is what our man makes of himself this month!

The Return of Diana Mars!

So many readers have wondered, "Where is Diana Mars?" This popular author took a break from writing, but we're excited that she's now writing for Silhouette Desire with *Peril in Paradise*.

Christmas in January!

For those of you who can't get enough of the holidays, please don't let Suzannah Davis's charming *A Christmas Cowboy* get away.

Mystery and Danger...

In Modean Moon's *Interrupted Honeymoon*.

Baby, Baby...

In Shawna Delacorte's *Miracle Baby*.

So start the New Year right with Silhouette Desire!

With all best wishes for a great 1995,

Lucia Macro
Senior Editor

Please address questions and book requests to:
Silhouette Reader Service
U.S.: 3010 Walden Ave., P.O. Box 1325, Buffalo, NY 14269
Canadian: P.O. Box 609, Fort Erie, Ont. L2A 5X3

SHAWNA DELACORTE
MIRACLE BABY

SILHOUETTE *Desire*®

Published by Silhouette Books

America's Publisher of Contemporary Romance

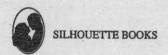

SILHOUETTE BOOKS

ISBN 0-373-05905-1

MIRACLE BABY

Copyright © 1995 by Sharon K. Dennison

This edition published by arrangement with Harlequin Enterprises B.V.

® and TM are trademarks of Harlequin Enterprises B.V., used under license. Trademarks indicated with ® are registered in the United States Patent and Trademark Office, the Canadian Trade Marks Office and in other countries.

Printed in U.S.A.

Books by Shawna Delacorte

Silhouette Desire

Sarah and the Stranger #730
The Bargain Bachelor #759
Cassie's Last Goodbye #814
Miracle Baby #905

SHAWNA DELACORTE

lives in Southern California, where she has worked for several years in television production. She has always enjoyed writing, but it was not until she switched from nonfiction to fiction that she felt she had found a happy home.

An avid photographer who loves to travel, Shawna laughs as she says, "You should see me getting on a plane—my laptop computer hanging from one shoulder, my camera bag hanging from the other shoulder and my purse somewhere in between. Sometimes I actually have to hold my boarding pass with my teeth."

One

"**H**ey, you there—Red!" An angry male voice shattered the morning quiet of the main street.

Darvi Stanton turned her head in the direction of the shout as she closed her car door. Her gaze lit on a tall man with a scraggly beard and shaggy hair. He was dressed in faded torn jeans and a wrinkled plaid shirt. His stance affirmed his challenge—one long leg on the ground, the other on the floorboard of his battered pickup truck, his hands squarely on his hips. She looked around to see if there was someone behind her who he might have been shouting at.

"Yeah, you with the red hair. You're in *my* parking place!"

She squinted in the morning sun and brought her hand to her forehead to shade her eyes. "Since my car is already parked here, I'd say the space is mine."

"Everyone in town knows that's where I always park."

She looked toward the parking space, then back at him. "This is a public space on a public street."

"Who the hell do you think you are?"

His angry question left no doubt that she had violated his sense of the order of things.

Sarcastically she replied, "I know who I am. Who are you?" Then she turned abruptly and walked away, indicating to one and all that as far as she was concerned, the conversation was over.

He stood in stunned silence, glaring at her back as she walked away from him. He watched her long, copper-colored French braid swing across her right shoulder before his gaze lingered on how her jeans hugged her hips and the curve of her bottom. His anger gave way to curiosity tinged with excitement as a surge of desire darted through his body. Then the woman in her late twenties, wearing a paint-spattered sweatshirt, disappeared into the art-supply shop.

Darvi tucked the package under her arm as she spoke to Amy Sutter. Amy and her husband, Frank, owned the art-supply shop. Frank also managed the lumber yard down the street. "You don't know how happy I am to see these paints. I was beginning to think they were never going to show up." She turned toward the door and called back over her shoulder, giving a smile and a friendly wave, "Thanks for phoning me as soon as they came in."

Her smile immediately faded when she spotted the man she had sparred with earlier leaning against the doorjamb, staring at her. She glared at him as she brushed past on her way out the door. No sooner had she exited the shop than she came to an abrupt halt, whirled around and met his smirking grin.

He raised an eyebrow as he cocked his head. He unfolded his arms from across his chest, stood up straight and stuck his hands in his pockets. "You have a problem, Red?"

He saw the fire flash from her large emerald eyes as she spoke through clenched teeth, her anger barely under control. "That piece of junk truck of yours is blocking my car. I want you to move it right now."

He kept his voice low, every word and inflection purposely chosen to bait her, as he said softly, "You want me to move it right now? I haven't finished my errands yet. I'm afraid I won't be able to move it for a while." With that, he turned and walked down the sidewalk toward the lumber yard.

She yelled after him, her frustration greater than her anger, "Don't you dare turn your back on me. Who do you think you are?"

The stranger turned back toward her, flashed an absolutely dazzling smile through the scraggly beard and mocked her earlier words. "I know who I am. Who are you?"

Darvi pulled her car into the parking lot of the inn located just south of town on a bluff overlooking the ocean. She glanced at her watch. She had always prided herself on her punctuality. She hated being late. Her temper flared as she thought about the incident earlier that morning. The man in the pickup truck had purposely kept her waiting fifteen minutes before he had let her out of the parking space.

She looked around the nearly deserted parking lot as she climbed out of her car and immediately recognized the large black sedan belonging to Carl Adamson. The other vehicle was a sleek red sports car she had never seen before.

Carl was not only the architect on the renovation project, he was also the owner of the property. He had personally hired her, overruling the recommendation of the contractor. She would be providing all the special stained-glass windows for the turn-of-the-century bed-and-breakfast inn on the Oregon coast. It was the largest project she had ever been contracted to do, and she was just a little nervous, even though she had full confidence in her capabilities.

As she entered the lobby she spotted Carl standing by the fireplace, talking with another man. She made her way toward them, offering an apologetic smile. "Carl, I'm so sorry to be late. Some scruffy, arrogant jerk blocked me into a parking space this morning with his beat-up old truck and wouldn't let me out." She turned briefly toward the other man, acknowledged his presence with a friendly smile and said hello.

Carl was a gracious, outgoing man in his early fifties, with dark hair graying slightly at the temples. "Don't give it another thought. I just got here myself. Let me introduce you to the contractor on this project. Darvi Stanton this is Rance Coulter. The two of you will be working closely together for the next few months so you'd better get to know each other."

Darvi extended her hand to Rance as she carefully looked him over. He was in his early thirties, had thick blond hair and clear blue eyes and stood about six feet three inches tall. The faint scar that started just below his lower lip and extended to his chin was the only flaw on an otherwise incredibly handsome face. He was dressed in designer jeans and a brightly patterned sweater that complemented his tanned features. There was something vaguely familiar about him, something around his eyes and nose, but she was not exactly sure what it was.

"I'm very pleased to meet you. I'm really looking forward to getting started on this. It's going to be a real challenge, but I think this will be quite a showplace when it's finished." Her enthusiasm for the project filled the air, but inside she felt apprehensive. Carl had told her that the contractor had completed several jobs over the past few years with someone in Portland who did stained glass. He had wanted to hire the same man for this job because he knew and trusted his abilities. Darvi realized she would have to work very hard to win his confidence.

Rance felt the soft warmth of her touch as he grasped her outstretched hand in his. He extended the same dazzling smile he had used earlier that day when he had confronted her on the street, not knowing at that time who she was. "Scruffy arrogant jerk? I'll admit that I certainly needed a shave and a haircut. I'd been tramping around in the wilderness for two weeks, then I spent another two weeks on the beach in Hawaii. My clothes were a mess, although no more so than that 'interesting' outfit of yours—but, arrogant jerk?"

His voice dripped with sarcasm. "Really, Red—you were the one who stole my parking space. And that 'beat-up old truck,' as you so callously called it, has great sentimental value." He had intended to put her on the defensive with his verbally aggressive manner. It was a tactic that usually worked to his advantage, especially with strangers. It gave him more time to size them up, to categorize them, to determine what tact to use in getting what he wanted. But he had woefully underestimated Darvi Stanton.

She glared at him, her eyes flashing defiantly. "Don't call me 'Red'!" Then she paused and blatantly scrutinized him. "I didn't recognize you all cleaned up. I'll take back the *scruffy,* but *arrogant* and *jerk* still seem applicable."

The dazzling smile faded from his face as he stared at her, his eyes locked with hers in silent combat. He stretched his tall frame to the maximum.

Darvi Stanton stood a little over five feet nine inches—tall men did not intimidate her. She refused to back down from his aggressive body language.

Carl broke the tense moment as he nervously cleared his throat and chuckled self-consciously. "You two seem to have gotten off to a bad start. You're going to have to get along better than this if we're going to complete these renovations on schedule." He stepped between them, placing a hand on each of their shoulders. "Now, why don't you two kiss and make up so we can get on with our business?"

Darvi shot Rance a tempestuous look, then turned her attention to Carl, giving him her best confidence-inducing smile. "I'm thoroughly professional. I never let my personal feelings interfere with my work." She glared at Rance again. "My portion of this project will be completed on schedule."

Rance silently admitted to a grudging admiration for the way she had stood up to his bullying. Maybe Carl's insistence on hiring her had not been such a bad idea after all. If her work was half as good as he claimed, this project could turn out to be something very special. Nonetheless, he was unable to resist one last dig. He cocked his head as he smiled at her. "Are you sure you don't want to kiss and make up? I'm willing to take a chance."

Darvi turned an expressionless face to Rance, perused his being, then dismissed him with a withering stare. But her disdain was only a facade. The sensation of his touch as their hands had clasped had sent tingles across her skin. She did not like the feelings he stirred in her. It was this discomfort that had caused her to be particularly antagonistic toward his comments.

Again Carl took charge, grabbing both of them by the arm and guiding them through the lobby to the wide curving staircase with the hand-carved banister that led to the second floor. "Come on, let's do a walk-through."

Darvi and Rance followed, neither saying anything.

When they reached the second floor Carl proceeded down the hall, addressing his comments more to Darvi than Rance. "As you know, there are twenty rooms with private baths, four corner suites with living room downstairs and bedroom upstairs, the entrance lobby and the dining room. Each room will be decorated in its own dominant color and style—no two rooms will be exactly the same." They walked through an opened doorway of one of the rooms. "This room is typical of most as far as size and floor plan are concerned."

Darvi made notes as Carl talked, absorbed with her own concerns and not paying any attention to Rance. They inspected one of the corner suites, then walked outside onto the large deck that extended from the entrance lobby to the edge of the cliff, overlooking the rocky shoreline.

Rance eyed Darvi intently as she leaned forward against the railing, watching the ocean waves crash against the rocks below. The sunlight caught the copper highlights of her hair. Her smooth, flawless skin emulated creamy silk. She wore very little makeup. He thought to himself how beautiful she was. He sensed something disturbing but could not pin down the feeling. He snapped out of his reverie as a frown furrowed his brow. *She's stubborn and exasperating. She certainly fits the stereotype of redheads having a feisty temper.*

Carl glanced at his watch. "I have an appointment in Summitville with a client who wants to discuss the design for an office building. I'd better run." He reached into his pocket, withdrew a key and handed it to Darvi. "Here, take this key to the front door. I'm sure there will be times you'll want to get in and out of here when the construction people aren't working." He looked at Rance, some ten feet away, sitting on the deck with his back against the railing, then at Darvi once more. "I'd like to see some preliminary sketches of the windows, including dimensions and color schemes, in two weeks. Is that okay with both of you?"

Darvi shot Rance a quick look then turned and smiled at Carl. "I don't have any problem with that." She glared at Rance. "How about you?"

He stood up, dusted off the seat of his jeans with his hands and smiled solicitously at her. "No problems here."

Carl shook hands with both of them. "Good. We'll meet again week after next. You two stay here as long as you need. Just don't forget to lock up when you leave."

After Carl left, Rance and Darvi said nothing at first as each cautiously assessed the other. Finally Darvi broke the silence. "I suppose we'd better exchange phone numbers. It sounds like we'll be seeing a lot of each other over the next few months." She turned to a clean page in her notepad, then looked at Rance— pencil poised.

He grinned and casually sauntered over to where she stood. "I wondered how long it would be before you wanted my phone number." He reached into his pocket and pulled out a business card with the information she had requested.

She turned the card over several times with her long delicate fingers then held it up in front of his face. "Don't flatter yourself, buster. This is strictly business." The scent of his after-shave excited her, a realization that made her uncomfortable. She reached into her large shoulder bag, pulled out one of her own business cards and handed it to him.

He took the card from her; he wanted to touch her, to run his fingertips across her cheek, but he restrained himself, refusing to give in to the temptation. He read the card, noting the address. "So, they finally rented the Vanowen studio. It's been vacant for six months." He looked her squarely in the eye. "You live in the back of the studio?"

Darvi nodded as the words stuck in her throat and her mouth went dry. His eyes seemed to be holding her in his power, exercising some sort of mystical control over her. With great difficulty, she broke their eye contact and stumbled backward a couple of steps.

Rance pocketed the card, then gazed out over the panoramic scene. He felt lost in thought, as if he were actually somewhere else. He finally returned his attention to Darvi. "I'll talk to you in a day or two. We can compare notes then. Right now I have lots to do. As I said, I've been out of town for the past month." He flashed one of those dazzling smiles of his. "That's how I missed your grand arrival in our fair community—" he paused, giving just the proper intonation to his words to ensure her irritation "—and why you didn't know about my parking space."

At the mention of the parking space, she stiffened. "You can take your parking space and... " She turned on her heel and stormed off, not bothering to finish her sentence.

He watched with amusement as she walked away. His amusement slowly faded and a smoldering intensity took its place as his gaze fixed on her retreating form. Rance slowly shook his head then walked back inside the building. The job of locking up the inn had fallen to him.

Darvi sat in her car, gripping the steering wheel so tightly her knuckles turned white. *What an infuriating man. How dare he talk to me that way. Humph! Insinuating that my asking for his phone number in any way implied a personal interest.* What bothered her even more than his arrogant attitude was the way he attracted her. With a project that would require all her time and energy and that had already gotten off to a bad start, she could not afford to be distracted by Rance Coulter. A hint of sadness crept over her. She could not afford to be distracted by any man—period—with or without the added pressure of an important job. Not ever again. Especially not with the agony that had lived inside her every minute of every day for the past two years.

* * *

Rance owned two acres of land on the outskirts of town. At the front of the property stood a comfortable country-style home and behind it, a large barn that had been converted into a woodworking shop. He pulled his red sports car into the garage, parking next to his old pickup truck, then entered the house from the garage and went immediately to his office.

Bill Jenkins, his construction foreman, had stopped by periodically during his absence to see that everything was all right. He had stacked four weeks' worth of mail on the desk. Rance settled back in the chair, picked up the first envelope and opened it.

Darvi fixed herself a quick dinner, then sat down at the work table in her studio. Hundreds of ideas whirled in her head. She wanted to get some sketches done while they were still fresh. She would then translate the sketches into watercolors, done to scale on heavy white paper. She preferred using watercolors for presentations because they projected the translucent quality of colored glass. She worked long into the night, so absorbed in the task at hand she was unaware of how much time was elapsing. It was after midnight when she stopped for the evening.

Passing through the sliding door that separated her studio from her bedroom was like stepping back into another century. There were silky fabrics, lace-edged feather pillows and gossamer veils. A large canopied bed occupied the center of the room, covered with a downy soft quilt and pillows. An excellent reproduction of the Tiffany Wisteria lamp sat on an antique oak nightstand, throwing subdued light across one corner of the room. The walls were hung with tapestries. A large antique oak dresser rested at the other end of the room. Clustered on top of it were numerous framed photographs, some old and others recent—all in antique frames nonetheless. The bedroom's muted colors of light and dark rose, pale mauve and pink, creamy ivory and beige hues, with various shades of blue bespoke a soft sensuality.

The bathroom contained large fluffy towels and throw rugs in the same muted shades as the bedroom. Scented bath oils and small perfumed soaps in flowered bowls sat on a ledge by the large old claw-foot bathtub.

Darvi quickly undressed and ran a tub of hot water. Her muscles ached from bending over the work table for so many hours without getting up to stretch. She added some jasmine-scented bath oil, then eased her body into the soothing water. A slight smile of contentment turned the corners of her mouth as she felt her muscles relax. Then, without warning or invitation, images of Rance Coulter began to dance across her closed eyelids. She quickly opened her eyes. Rance Coulter was definitely not the last thing she wanted on her mind before going to bed.

Darvi awoke with a start. She sensed it was late, much later than she wanted it to be. She focused on the clock, then threw off the covers and sat up. She had planned on being up by six. She had overslept by almost two hours.

At eight-thirty Darvi pulled into the parking lot at the inn and immediately spotted Rance's old truck. She grabbed her large shoulder bag and proceeded to the inn, where she made her way across the lobby, shuffling through sawdust and wood chips, sidestepping stacked boards of various lengths, bypassing boxes of ceramic tile and numerous construction tools. Sounds of hammering and power saws came from down the hall. Somewhere a radio was tuned to a rock station. She quickly headed for the staircase and the second floor, relieved that Rance was nowhere in sight. As she approached the top of the stairs he suddenly appeared from out of nowhere and stepped in front of her, effectively blocking her path.

He studied her. Like the day before, she wore old jeans and a sweatshirt. Her long copper-colored hair was pulled back in a French braid. She smelled faintly of some tantalizing fragrance he could not quite place. He purposely made an elaborate display of looking at his watch, then shaking his head disapprovingly at her.

He caught the quick look of guilt that darted across her face as she spoke.

"I'd planned to be here by seven o'clock, but I stayed up too late and overslept."

"Oh? And just what is it you were doing that kept you awake so late? Some of us are able to handle a social life and still take care of business the next morning." He gleefully noticed the embarrassment his comments caused. His moment of triumph did not last long, though.

"My social life is none of your business." Her eyes flashed her anger. She stepped up to the landing at the top of the stairs, refusing to give him the psychological advantage of towering over her. They glared at each other, locked in a silent battle of wills.

Rance withdrew his other hand from behind his back and plopped a hard hat on top of her head. "This is a construction zone, Red. Hard hats must be worn at all times. Now, to business. Do you have any information for me yet? Any hint you might like to give me as to what size your windows are going to be and where you think you might like them installed?''

Darvi took a deep breath to calm her mounting irritation. She had to make an attempt to get along with this infuriating man. Her voice was strained, but she managed to keep out her anger. "I asked you not to call me 'Red.'"

A mischievous grin played at the corners of his mouth. "So you did ... so you did. However, that doesn't answer my question."

Darvi adopted a solicitous manner and replied in her most condescending tone of voice, "I have some of my sketches completed now." A quick look of surprise crossed his face, causing a satisfied smile to turn the corners of her mouth. "That's what *I* did last night." She brushed past him and walked down the hall. "Now, if you'll excuse me, I have work to do."

She felt slightly guilty about exaggerating the amount of work she had completed. She had a couple of sketches that satisfied her, but she was far from finished.

Rance watched as she entered one of the rooms. *She's the most exasperating woman I've ever met. Still, there's something about her...* He turned and went downstairs, preferring to leave his thought unfinished.

Once he was satisfied that Bill Jenkins had things under control, he left to take care of personal business. His refrigerator was empty, he had laundry to do and he needed to talk to Bobby Spencer about helping him with a special project for the inn renovations.

Bobby was Amy Sutter's nineteen-year-old nephew. He lived in the small apartment above Amy and

Frank's garage and worked part-time for Amy in the art-supply shop, earning just enough to pay for his classes at the art center and have a little spending money. When classes were not in session he usually went back to his parents' home in Medford, Oregon—unless Rance needed his help with some new job.

Bobby was a wiz at woodworking. He enjoyed helping Rance make special doors with inlaid wood patterns, and Rance was only too happy to pay him for his assistance.

Custom woodwork was Rance's specialty. His father had been a master carpenter and cabinet maker, and he had learned the skills from him. Even though Rance now had a contractor's license, he still enjoyed doing custom woodwork. He had made some furniture pieces, but his favorites were the patterned doors and the inlaid dining room table and coffee table tops.

As soon as he had heard Carl's ideas and studied the blueprints for the inn renovations, Rance had pitched the idea of using patterned wooden doors on each of the rooms. Like the stained-glass windows, each door would be different. Carl had liked the idea, but only if the patterns on the doors related to the patterns in the stained-glass windows so the room decor would feel cohesive. Rance had agreed, but now he was not so sure. It meant he would be working closer with Darvi than he would have otherwise.

Darvi and Rance did not see each other for the next three days. She worked on her sketches, translated them into watercolors and figured out window dimensions so she could supply Rance with the information he needed. But the task that presented her with the greatest difficulty was keeping her mind from wandering to thoughts of him.

For his part, Rance spent much of his time in his workshop designing the patterns for the doors he would make. With the day-to-day activities at the construction site in the capable hands of Bill Jenkins, he had more time to devote to this project. As soon as he figured out the patterns and decided which types of wood he wanted to use, Bobby could start cutting the individual pieces of wood to size.

Darvi left the art-supply shop on Saturday afternoon. As she approached her car, she saw a piece of paper stuck under her windshield wiper. She scanned the note. *You're in my parking space again!* She looked up and saw Rance leaning against the street sign post, watching her.

As soon as he was confident she had seen him, he strolled over to where she stood. "This makes twice, Red."

His voice was soft and intimate, yet still managed to convey the arrogance she had originally associated with him.

"One more time and I might be forced to have your car towed." He allowed a brief moment of serious reflection as he reached out and almost touched her cheek. He quickly withdrew his hand before his fingers actually came in contact with her skin.

His brief, but abrupt change in demeanor confused her. It was almost as if he had permitted her to glimpse the real him through a chink in his armor of arrogance. She quickly shook off her confusion and shoved the note into his shirt pocket. "Don't you even think about it!"

Two

For the next few days they seemed to be running into each other constantly, even though she was not at the construction site—there were the dry cleaners, the drugstore, the gas station and once at a stoplight. Rance would be marginally polite and Darvi would be reserved as they exchanged greetings. Each encounter left her in a state of quivering confusion. Rance Coulter had an extremely disconcerting effect on her and she did not like it.

Darvi struggled with two bags of groceries as she carried them across the parking lot toward her car. She felt one of the bags slip from her hands. In an effort to keep it from falling, she lost her grip on the other bag, as well.

"I've got them."

She jumped at the sound of the smooth masculine voice directly behind her. She turned around and found herself looking into Rance's face. She was flustered, her normally controlled manner slightly shaken. "Where did you come from?"

He seized on her obvious discomfort and continued to bait her. "Where did I come from? Well, I was born and raised in Portland, then—"

"You know that's not what I meant!" Her words burst out in a flash of anger tempered with just a hint of wariness. "Why were you standing behind me? Are you following me?"

He had been waiting for the opportunity to use her own words on her. "Don't flatter yourself, Red."

She felt the heat of embarrassment start across her cheeks. "I didn't mean—"

"You really should have used a cart rather than trying to carry two bags full of..." He looked inside one of the bags and saw a carton of eggs and two glass jars. "A bag of breakable things."

"You're right." Her manner softened, became almost shy, in spite of his attitude. "Thanks for rescuing me... I mean, rescuing my groceries." She reached for one of the bags, but he refused to relinquish it.

"I'd better carry them to make sure they get safely to your car."

When they reached the vehicle she opened the trunk and he set the bags inside. "Thanks."

He smiled at her as his blue eyes took on a meaningful look, and lightly touched her cheek with his fingertips. "It was my pleasure."

Darvi set her large shoulder bag on the floor, then stepped out onto the second-floor balcony of one of the corner suites. The day was remarkably clear. The sun shone brightly, creating jeweled points of light on the ocean's surface. She closed her eyes and tilted her head back, allowing the warmth of the sun's rays to wash over her face. A contented smile played across her mouth as she slowly ran her tongue over her upper lip. The gentle ocean breeze caught a loose tendril of hair and brushed it against her cheek.

Rance stood just inside the balcony door, watching her, an uncomfortable amount of intensity shoving at his consciousness. He marveled at the texture and quality of her skin, the finely sculpted features of her beautiful face, the curve of her neck, her long delicate fingers resting on the balcony railing. He watched her flick her tongue across her lip. He briefly tried to visualize what she would look like with her French braid combed out and her hair flowing over her shoulders. *How can someone that exasperating be so desirable?*

He shook his head. He was unhappy with the errant thought that had, again, forced its way into his consciousness. He stepped out onto the balcony as he spoke. "Sorry to interrupt a quiet moment of reflection..."

Darvi whirled around as the sound of a male voice broke into her thoughts. As soon as she focused on Rance she relaxed and gave him a shy smile. "You startled me. I guess I was daydreaming. I didn't hear you come into the room."

He held her gaze, her eyes were alert, questioning.

"I was just going to suggest that we compare notes before proceeding any further."

He saw something flit tnrough her eyes, but it was gone before he could read it.

A twinge of guilt poked at her. He was obviously proffering an olive branch of sorts, making an attempt to get along. It was what she should have done, rather than allowing herself to become irritated by his remarks. Yet there was something about him that seemed to always activate her defenses. She offered him a sincere smile. "Sure, that would be fine. When do you want to do it?"

"I have some business to take care of right now. How about one-thirty this afternoon downstairs in the lobby?"

"Sure, that's fine with me."

As he left the balcony, Rance called over his shoulder, "See you later."

Darvi worked uninterrupted for the rest of the morning, grabbed a quick bite of lunch, then was back at the inn for her one-thirty meeting with Rance. She nervously paced up and down the lobby as she glanced at her watch. It was one forty-five—Rance was late. She leaned back against the fireplace and drummed her fingers on the mantel as irritation over his tardiness built inside her. She would give him fifteen minutes more. If he had not shown up by then, she would leave.

Fifteen minutes later she pulled out of the parking lot. Three blocks down the street she spotted Rance standing on a corner, talking with two other men.

He looked up at the sound of screeching tires and saw Darvi's car come to a halt at the curb. He glanced at his watch. An involuntary frown wrinkled his brow as he walked over to her and leaned against the car door. He smiled apologetically. "I was on my way when I got sidetracked. We have a softball game this Saturday and the guys were—"

"You can stay sidetracked for the rest of the day as far as I'm concerned."

* * *

Darvi was just finishing up the dinner dishes when she heard the bell at the front of the studio. She grabbed a towel and dried her hands as she went to answer the door.

"I should have been paying more attention to the time earlier today." Rance flashed her his best "please forgive me" smile. "Mind if I come in?"

She hesitated a moment, then stepped aside.

"I really need to get window dimensions from you and some kind of layout showing where you want them installed. We also need to compare designs for windows and doors to make sure we're on the right track. Time is running out. I have some patterns for the doors and some wood samples." He held up his carrying case, cocked his head, raised an eyebrow and issued a verbal challenge. "I'll show you mine if you show me yours." He caught her look of wariness, and immediately assumed a pleasant, but businesslike, attitude as he continued, "We could kick around some ideas if you're not too busy. I want to get Bobby started on cutting the wood pieces."

Her smile was gracious, but her manner remained cautious. "Sure, now is as good a time as any. My sketches are in back." Darvi started toward the rear of the studio. He followed her. She stepped through the sliding door and pulled it closed behind her, but it did not shut completely. He opened the door and entered the bedroom.

Rance stood in stunned silence as he surveyed the surroundings—the muted colors, the soft fabrics, the large canopied bed. He slowly moved about the room, picking up objects, then setting them back down. He touched the things he could not pick up, felt textures, inhaled the many floral and spicy fragrances.

Darvi stood in the corner of the room by the oak dresser, glued to the spot, as she watched him wander around her bedroom. Anxiety churned in the pit of her stomach. The expression on his face was disarming. He seemed to be carefully studying her private retreat, analyzing her through her chosen environment.

The surprise in his tone of voice was unmistakable. "I never would have guessed it. You're a closet romantic. Under all that anger, tough talk and defensiveness—" he waved his arm around the room "—is this. I'm truly amazed."

He sat on the edge of her bed, bounced up and down, then stood up again. "Nice bed. Feels comfortable." His gaze landed on something silky on top of a lace-trimmed pillow at the head of the bed. He reached for it and his hand closed over a camisole and tap pants. He looked at her again and allowed the barest hint of a lascivious grin. "No sirree, I never would have guessed."

The faint fragrance of roses—he could not tell if it was bath oil or perfume—wafted across his nostrils. He held up the camisole by its shoulder straps. "Who would have thought that something like this would be hiding under those faded jeans and paint-spattered sweatshirts of yours?"

Darvi saw the look come into his eyes as their color changed from a clear blue to more of a smoky hue. A shiver darted up her spine. Anxiety welled inside her, a feeling she immediately covered with her defense mechanism—anger. "I don't believe there's anything in my bedroom that's any of your business." She snatched the garments out of his hand. "And I'll thank you to stop drooling over my lingerie!"

She glared at him until her anger gave way to embarrassment. They stood very close, their gazes magnetically locked. Only the sound of breathing, both his and hers, intruded upon the stillness of the room. Panic raced through her as she said in a quiet, quavering voice—no longer the angry, self-assured person of a few minutes earlier, "Please wait in the studio. I'll get the sketches and be right out."

A note of caution sounded loud and clear inside his head. He sensed her panic, but was confused about what had frightened her. He had categorized her as a tough, in-charge person—someone who knew the score and could take care of herself. What he had just glimpsed was a vulnerable and frightened woman.

Rance answered her, his voice not as steady as he would have liked, "Sure. I'll wait in the studio." He started to leave, then turned back toward her. He began to say something, then changed his mind. He left the room, sliding the door closed behind him.

Trembling, Darvie sank into the softness of the bed. She gulped in several deep breaths as she tried to calm herself. That look that had come into Rance's eyes had frightened her. Not because of what he might do, but because of the emotions he had stirred in her. They were things she did not want to feel. He had blasted a hole right through her carefully constructed facade without even trying. She felt the wall crumbling, the panic rising within her. He frightened her...not physically, but certainly emotionally.

Rance was in the studio, unpacking his case, when Darvi returned. He paused to watch her as she walked toward him. He studied her for a moment, his expression questioning.

She returned his look, trying to project a casual air. "Is there a problem?"

He spoke hesitantly. "No...I guess not." He continued to look at the uncertainty in her eyes. "Are you all right?"

She glanced down at the floor and then across the room, unable to meet his gaze. "Yes, of course. Why wouldn't I—"

He placed his hands tentatively on her shoulders, turning her so she faced him. He kept her at arm's length. "Look, I didn't mean to upset you. It was just some harmless teasing...." He allowed his gaze to drop to the floor as his voice trailed off. He spoke more to himself than to her, "At least, I thought it was harmless."

He felt her tensed muscles begin to relax, her defenses lower a little. She told him softly, "It's okay. I...I just overreacted, that's all."

They looked into each other's eyes for a long moment, then Rance suddenly dropped his hands from her shoulders and stepped back. Now it was his turn to panic. Something about her had touched him. He felt himself being drawn to her, wanting to protect her, wanting to take care of her—wanting to kiss away whatever fears were hiding in the dark corners of her mind. The last thing he wanted or needed was a relationship—a commitment to anyone. *It's either business or a casual affair...and I don't think she's the casual-affair type.*

Relationships were vastly overrated as far as Rance was concerned. They were not for him, at least not anymore. He and Joan had been married for seven disastrous months when he was twenty-two. She ended up running off with the man she had been dating prior to Rance. That had been ten years ago. He had neither seen her nor heard from her since. He had gotten a divorce and had tried to put the entire incident behind him, but the emotional scars still ran deep. Since that time his choice in women had tended toward those with the same "no strings attached" philosophy as his own.

Rance turned back toward his patterns and wood samples. "Let's see if we can't get some work done before it gets too late."

Darvi was grateful he had removed his hands from her shoulders. A little over a week ago she had no idea who Rance Coulter was. She knew he was the contractor for the renovations, but she had never set eyes on him. Now he caused her to feel things she did not want to feel. Unanswered stirrings forced themselves into her consciousness.

She tried to shake off the awkwardness and adopt an upbeat attitude. "Would you like something to drink? I have coffee, iced tea, soft drinks."

A sheepish grin spread across his face. "I don't suppose you'd have a cold beer handy, would you?"

"I do if you're not picky about the brand." She started toward the refrigerator as she continued to talk. "Amy was over last week. She drinks beer, so I bought a six-pack. There are four bottles left." She returned with an opened bottle and handed it to him. "Would you like a glass?"

"No, this is fine. Thanks." He took a swallow, and noticed she had not brought a bottle for herself. "You don't drink beer?"

She scrunched up her nose and made a face, indicating her distaste, then she started laughing. "No, I never acquired a taste for it. I'm more of a wine person."

"I like wine, too—usually with dinner. It's nice to know we have something in common," he allowed a wry grin, "other than my parking space." He saw her anger start to flash, but just as quickly it disappeared. He turned serious for a moment. "It's also nice to see you smile, to see you're not always so uptight, angry and defensive."

A slight flush came to her cheeks as a shy smile curled the corners of her mouth. "Well, it's nice to see that *you're* not always an insufferable, arrogant jerk."

He reached out and brushed an errant tendril of hair from her cheek. His fingertips lingered. Their eyes locked. An eerie stillness filled the air. Darvi could feel her heart pounding, hear the blood rushing in her ears. Her mouth and throat went dry as she tried to swallow. She felt the tremors start deep inside, then quickly spread through her body. She saw his eyes turn a smoky blue.

Rance was having difficulty breathing, as if the oxygen had been sucked from the room. He saw a multitude of fearful emotions darting through her eyes—anxiety, nervousness, uncertainty, panic—yet underlying the fear was a soft sensuality. He sensed a passion buried in the very depths of her soul, a passion that threatened to burst forth. He felt his self-control wavering, teetering on the edge of abandonment. He slowly leaned his face into hers, his gaze fixed on her mouth.

She hesitated for a brief moment, not at all sure what to do, then pulled back from him. Her voice, when she spoke, had a sharpness. "I think we'd better get to work before the evening is gone."

He looked at her questioningly, then assumed a businesslike attitude. "I think you're right. My primary concern at this time is dimensions rather than design and color."

"Could we talk color and design for a minute? The dimensions I have right now won't mean anything if I have to redo designs, because that will probably change the size of the windows."

He looked at her for a moment. "All right, that makes sense. What have you got?"

Darvi spread out sketches across her work table, some still line drawings, others transferred to watercolor. "I want to stay away from bright blue, bright green and bright red. I don't want this to look like the windows in some sixteenth-century European cathedral. I want to do something modern, yet reminiscent of the softness and sensuality of a time gone by. I want muted colors—nothing that will keep anyone awake at night."

He gazed at her in amazement. "That's incredible. That's exactly what I was thinking—soft colors with a Victorian feel."

His words of approval sent a flush through her as she continued, "I want the windows to be representative of the view from the room—the ocean-view rooms will depict ocean scenes and the mountain-view rooms will have mountain and forest scenes. I'm going to limit the designs to four colors. Each room will have a different dominant color, yet combine all four colors. That way the various colors of sheets, towels and things like that can be switched from room to room without interrupting the overall flow."

Rance slowly nodded approvingly. "I had my
doubts last week—I even had my doubts this morning. But I think we'll be able to work together just
fine." His gaze captured hers for a brief moment. He
saw the enthusiasm she felt for her work glowing in her
eyes. He picked up a couple of her sketches, a slight
frown wrinkling his brow. "Some of these windows
are unusual shapes and sizes." He held up a triangu-
lar-shaped design and another one that was a narrow
oval. "I didn't realize you were planning on using irregular sizes and odd geometric shapes, rather than
standard dimensions."

"Is that going to be a problem?" Her concern was
genuine. "I hadn't considered that aspect. Maybe..."
She hesitated, not sure how much to compromise her
creativity. "Maybe I could try to fit the designs into a
more conventional shape."

"No... " His voice trailed off as he studied more
of her drawings. "No, I think we'll be okay. The way
you've done this will enhance the room much more
than the traditional rectangular shape." He returned
his gaze to her. "However, this does mean you'll have
to firm up your specifications as soon as possible so I
can get the necessary changes to Carl so he can revise
the blueprints. I'll also need to adjust some of my
patterns for the doors to coincide with the geometric
shapes you've chosen."

"Could I see some of your door ideas?"

He pulled out some patterns and wood samples.

Darvi studied the sketches, then picked up a presentation piece he had mounted on plywood. It was
heavy, but she was accustomed to working with heavy
glass and windows and had no trouble propping it up
against the wall. It was a tabletop design, five differ-

ent types of wood inlaid in an intricate pattern and polished to a smooth finish.

Her voice conveyed her surprise. "This is beautiful." She turned to face him. "Do you do this type of custom woodwork all the time?"

"Not as often as I'd like."

She returned her attention to the design sample, running her fingers across the smooth surface of the wood. "I'm very impressed."

His voice took on a softness. "Thank you." Then he quickly regained his business attitude. "I didn't bring any of the construction blueprints with me, so why don't we call it a night and meet at the inn early tomorrow morning? We can do a walk-through and mark the exact location you want each window installed." He rose from his chair, stretched his tall frame and gathered his sketches.

Darvi stood up, too. "That sounds great. I don't have all the sizes and shapes set yet, but I will at least be able to give you the approximate dimensions on all the windows. I don't want to hold you up so, as far as the other windows are concerned, we can go ahead and determine size and shape. I'll design something to fit. Shall we meet about seven o'clock in the morning?"

"Perfect. See you then." He looked into her eyes. He noticed that the panic and anxiety had disappeared, but the nervousness and uncertainty still lingered. His gaze dropped to her mouth. He wanted to calm that nervousness, to kiss away the uncertainty. He wanted to leave her studio before he tried, once again, to do just that. "Good night, Darvi."

"Good night." She closed and locked the studio door, then turned out the light before walking to her bedroom.

Rance sat in his car in front of her studio, not sure exactly what he was feeling. He did know it was something different, something special. He found Darvi Stanton to be an enigma. On the surface she was hot tempered, exasperating and stubborn. It seemed they had spent most of their time together clashing over something.

Yet he sensed a different person underneath—a vulnerable, yet sensual, woman who had chosen to hide behind a shell. As he started his car and drove home he pondered just what it was that could be so painful she would choose to hide behind such a tough exterior.

Darvi closed the bedroom door behind her and leaned against it as she surveyed the room. She loved this room. She had decorated it exactly the same as her old room in her oceanfront studio in Laguna Beach. When she made the decision to move from Southern California to Sandy Cove, Oregon, her one priority was finding a studio with the same type of living quarters. An angry frown crossed her face. And tonight this room—her sanctuary—had been invaded. How dare that insensitive, selfish, lying, loathsome—

She froze in horror as she realized it was not Rance Coulter she had just described, but *Jerry Peterson*. A violent shiver shot through her body at the mere thought of him. Her stomach churned. She felt physically ill. Darvi wanted nothing more from life than to permanently erase the despicable Jerry Peterson from her consciousness for all time.

She flopped down across the bed and squeezed her eyes shut in an attempt to drive away the torment. Exhaustion finally overcame her and she fell into an uneasy sleep. A recurring nightmare played through her mind until she could stand it no longer. She awoke with a start, sitting bolt upright in her bed. Beads of perspiration dotted her face. Her breathing was labored and her heart pounded. She still wore the clothes from the night before. The clock in the other room chimed five times. She reluctantly climbed out of bed and trudged into the bathroom.

At exactly seven o'clock Darvi pulled into the parking lot of the inn. She spotted Rance's truck along with the vehicles belonging to some of the construction crew. She grabbed her large shoulder bag and headed for the door. As she crossed the lobby, Rance called to her from the deck, "Out here."

She stepped onto the deck and a smile immediately spread across her face. Her voice was filled with warmth as she spoke. "How delightful!"

He had taken one of the discarded doors and set it up on two sawhorses to make a table. The makeshift table held a thermos filled with steaming coffee, two mugs and a paper sack containing fresh croissants—still warm from the bakery. Two crates posed as chairs.

He returned her smile. "I hope you take your coffee black. I don't have any cream or sugar."

"Black is perfect, thank you." She sat down on one of the crates. "What made you think of this?"

"It was nothing special." He poured hot coffee into the mugs and set one in front of her. "It was just my own natural creative brilliance."

Darvi took a sip of her coffee, not at all sure if his comments were said in jest or whether he was serious. She decided, for the sake of peaceful coexistence, that she would treat the remark as a joke. "I'll give you points for this one."

Rance captured her gaze with his. He searched her eyes, trying to see beyond the wall she had placed between herself and the rest of the world. He sat on the edge of the sawhorse next to her. "Darvi, what's wrong?" His gaze traveled across her face, then settled on her eyes again. She squirmed uncomfortably as their eyes locked. "What frightens you so much? What are you hiding from?"

He saw the shock, then the fear, flicker through her eyes before she turned her face away. He watched as her gaze darted across the panoramic ocean scene, nervously seeking out something—what, he did not know. The silence that surrounded them grew louder and louder, until it had completely engulfed them, even shutting out the sounds of hammers and saws coming from inside the building.

He reached out and placed his fingertips under her chin and turned her face toward him, lifting until he could look into her eyes. He studied her for a moment then spoke very softly. "I'm a good listener— really I am." He offered her a sincere smile of encouragement. The indecision and confusion going on inside her were mirrored on her face, reflected in her eyes. He sensed she had been carrying a terrible burden for much too long. He thought she was on the verge of opening up, when suddenly everything changed.

The defensive wall went up again. She said tersely, "What is this, Psychology 101? Do you write a paper and turn it in at the end of the week? For your information, nothing's bothering me. I'm just fine."

She tried to glare at him, but was unable to hold his look. She turned away, but not before he glimpsed the pain that darted through her eyes.

He sat silently for a moment then stood up. His face might not have given any hint of his thoughts, but his tone of voice had a harsh edge, clearly indicating he did not believe a word she had said. "My mistake." He picked up the bakery sack and held it out. "Here, have one of these croissants. The bakery on Main Street makes them fresh every morning. They're really very good."

Darvi glanced at the sack, then at Rance, and helped herself to one of the rolls. "They do look good." She gazed at the ground as the guilt stabbed at her. "I didn't mean to snap at you like that." She drank the last swallow of her coffee. "I guess I'm a little tired. I didn't have a very good night's sleep." She held up her empty mug and smiled at him. "I'll take a refill, if there's any left."

"There's plenty."

They sat in silence, sipping their coffee and munching on their croissants. When they had finished the last of the coffee Rance gathered up the napkins and the empty paper bag and threw them in the large Dumpster. He picked up the thermos and mugs, paused briefly, then sat down on the sawhorse. "My offer still holds—I'm a good listener."

Darvi eyed him for a long moment, then looked away. "We should get to work. This is business, remember?"

He stood up, his manner brisk and his words clipped. "Right you are—this is business."

Three

———

Rance checked his watch. "It's five-thirty. The construction crew went home an hour and a half ago. What do you say we call it a day?" He started gathering up blueprints, sketches and the numerous notes he had made during the day. "I don't know about you, but I'm starved. We worked right through lunch and now it's dinnertime." He studied her for a moment, as if trying to make up his mind about something. His words were tentative. "Would you like to get something to eat?"

"I don't know..."

He saw the uncertainty come into her eyes, triggering an outburst of irritation on his part. "For crying out loud, Red. I'm just talking about grabbing a bite to eat. I'm not asking you to be the mother of my children." The words had come out of his mouth before he could stop them. Children were not a subject

he cared to discuss at all and certainly not with someone who had a very definite, albeit confusing, effect
on his senses.

Her anger flared to match his outburst. "I told you
not to call me 'Red'! I don't want to have to tell you
again." She glared at him for what seemed like eter-
nity before she had to look away. "The mother of my
children" were the last words she wanted to hear from
anyone, least of all Rance Coulter.

He knew he had been out of line. It was because he
felt a real attraction to her and it bothered him. It was
not the same as with other women. It had a whole
different feel to it. He took a steadying breath and
carefully measured his words. "I'll tell you what—why
don't we think of it as two business associates having
a business meal together."

She was not sure exactly where the conversation was
going. "I suppose that would be all right."

"Then it's settled." He finished putting his papers
into his case and they walked outside together. "I want
to go home first and get cleaned up. Do you want to
meet me at the Wine Bistro at seven o'clock?" He
paused, then cautiously ventured, "Or would you
prefer that I pick you up at your place?"

She hesitated a moment as she turned the idea over
in her mind. "I'll just meet you there—that would be
better." Having him pick her up at her place was not
the problem. What she wanted to avoid was an awk-
ward situation when he took her home. She felt
crowded, as if he were pressing her too much, trying
to pry into her personal life. The previous night he had
even started to kiss her. She wanted to do this job, be
professionally involved, but remain personally unin-
volved. She wanted Rance Coulter to stay out of her

personal life. What she would not admit, did not want to face, was her desire for exactly the opposite—for Rance Coulter to become an important part of her personal life.

"I'll see you at seven o'clock." Rance headed for the parking lot as he called back to her, unable to resist getting in one last taunt, "And try to be on time, Red. Okay?"

She shouted at him, her anger again flaring in response to his arrogance, "I'm not the one who has a problem with punctuality!" She gave it all the volume she had. "And don't call me 'Red'!" She watched as he climbed in his truck and drove off. Humph! The arrogance of the man was unbelievable. *I don't even know why I agreed to this.* She knew... deep down inside she knew exactly why. She was drawn to him like the moth to the flame.

Following dinner, Rance escorted Darvi across the street from the Wine Bistro to the Seaside Art Gallery. The gallery was open late that evening for a special showing of the latest works of a famous painter who had gotten his start as a local street artist. The exhibition was crowded and the champagne seemed to flow nonstop.

Rance watched her as Darvi studied one of the paintings. She was wearing a pair of silk slacks with a matching blouse. He had immediately been struck by the beautiful emerald green color that exactly matched her eyes. She wore a delicate gold chain around her neck and a matching gold bracelet. As they had been from the time he had first seen her, her long copper tresses were pulled back in a French braid.

He took two glasses of champagne from the tray and handed one to Darvi. She smiled politely as she accepted the glass. Again, he allowed a quick fantasy of what she would look like with her hair combed out, flowing over her shoulders—or possibly fanned out across a pillow as she lay...

He refused to complete the thought.

They made their way around the gallery, inspecting each painting. She kept the conversation on work. He noticed a wary, uncertain look come into her eyes every time he tried to talk to her about anything personal. When he asked where she came from, she told him Laguna Beach, but would not elaborate. He asked why she had left sunny Southern California for rainy Oregon, and she mumbled something about California getting too crowded, but basically evaded the question. He asked about her family. He had seen all the photographs in her bedroom and assumed it was a safe topic. She changed the subject without answering.

Rance felt the frustration building inside him. What had started simply had evolved into a genuine need, almost an obsession, to know more about her. What could have caused so much anger and defensiveness? He grabbed Darvi's hand and led her toward the back door. "It's very warm in here. Let's step outside and get some fresh air."

It was a beautiful night. She took in a deep breath as they stepped out onto the patio, then slowly expelled it. Before she was aware of what he was doing, Rance had pulled her into his arms. The silvery shimmer from the full moon highlighted his handsome features. He held her close, but not too close. A tremor shot through her. His touch was inviting. His after-shave tickled her senses. She felt her carefully constructed facade crumbling.

For a brief moment she did not care. Darvi melted into his arms as he drew her closer. She felt the hardness of his taut body as he held her. It had been a long time since she had allowed herself to experience the sensations that coursed through her. He excited her senses, made her blood race. It felt so right in his arms, she did not want to leave. She rested her head against his shoulder and closed her eyes. For a stilled moment in time she allowed herself to become part of him.

Rance felt her head against her shoulder and felt the tension suddenly drain from her body. It was as if she had decided to stop fighting. It so surprised him that he almost stumbled backward a step. She was soft and warm in his arms. He felt the firm fullness of her breasts pressing against his chest and an image of the silky camisole flashed through his mind.

It was Darvi who regained her senses and withdrew from his embrace. "I... It's late and I believe I've had enough fresh air." Her voice was slightly husky. In spite of the cool air, her face felt hot. She saw the smoky blue change come into his eyes as they held each other's looks.

"I believe you're right. It's probably time to call it a night." There was a touch of huskiness in his voice, too. The insistent whisper of the ocean waves in the background together with the light scent of her perfume tickled his already overstimulated senses. In a totally impulsive gesture he wrapped his arms around her again and captured her mouth. As soon as he tasted her soft lips, what started as a simple kiss quickly escalated. He felt her passion as she responded to his kiss, but it lasted only a moment before she jerked back from him.

Darvi's reply was defensive, her words angry. "What do you think you're doing?"

His retort was laced with sarcasm. "If you don't know then I must be doing it wrong."

"You know what I mean."

Rance leaned back against the wall and studied her a moment. "I was kissing you. I thought you wanted me to kiss you." He took a calming breath. "I know I wanted to kiss you."

Her defensiveness flared into anger and she pushed by him. "When I want you to kiss me, I'll let you know."

He watched as she stormed through the art gallery and out the front door. He had not meant for it to happen this way. He let the cool ocean breeze soothe his confusion. Could he have been that wrong about her body language? He did not think so. He felt her heated response before she retreated behind her facade.

Darvi sat in her car across the street in the Wine Bistro parking lot. Tears rolled down her cheeks as she tried to control her emotions. His kiss had stirred something deep inside her. She wanted to respond, had started to respond to his kiss and her desires. Then her fears had taken over and she slammed the door he had opened into her inner being.

She turned the key in the car's ignition and drove home. Her senses reeled from the inner battle that raged between her desire for Rance Coulter and her fear of how and what he made her feel. A bigger fear, all-consuming, was how he would feel about her if he ever found out the dark secret of her past. Did she dare take that chance?

Sleep eluded Rance as he thought about Darvi Stanton. One moment she was nestled warmly in his arms, her head resting tenderly on his shoulder; the next moment she was hurling her anger at him. He was accustomed to having his pick of women without having to put up with all the clutter. That was the way he wanted it—no promises, no commitments. He wondered if she was really worth all the trouble it would take to break through that wall she hid behind, to find the real Darvi. Was there someone truly special behind that wall?

Brief images of Darvi flashed through his mind— her dazzling smile when Carl introduced them before she realized who he was, the great enthusiasm and dedication she showed for her work, the frightened uncertain look in her eyes when he had teased her in her bedroom, the soft warmth of her body nestled in his arms and the momentary flash of fiery passion as she started to return his kiss. He decided there was, indeed, someone very special hiding in there. He finally fell asleep, delectable yet disturbing thoughts of Darvi Stanton filling his dreams.

Darvi stayed in bed the next morning. She had spent a restless night tossing and turning. She was more than simply tired, she was exhausted, as if she had been doing heavy physical labor for many hours. Her fingers moved slowly across her lips as the memory of Rance's kiss flooded her being. His lips were soft, his mouth very sensual. He had simply set her soul on fire in a matter of seconds. She had not been prepared for that, his kiss caught her totally by surprise.

She closed her eyes and visualized his commanding presence as he had leaned against the wall outside the art gallery, his handsome features highlighted by the silvery glow of the full moon. She quickly opened her eyes and shook her head to clear it of the image. She stared up at the canopy of flowered material above her head, then sighed and forced herself out of bed.

Just as Darvi was pulling the last stroke of her brush through her hair her phone rang. "Amy! This is a surprise. Did I forget to pay for something?"

Amy laughed in her typical outgoing good-natured way. "No, don't be silly. Nothing like that. It's the start of local softball season. The first game is this afternoon at one o'clock. Frank's going to be playing, so I thought I'd invite you to watch the game with me. Since you're new to Sandy Cove I didn't know if you understood that everyone's invited."

Darvi crinkled her nose and furrowed her brow in thought. "Softball? Sounds like fun. I'd love to."

"Good. We'll pick you up at noon. We always have a picnic after the game. Think you could make potato salad for about a dozen people?"

Darvi's eyes grew wide. "A dozen people? By noon?"

Amy's enthusiasm waned a bit. "Is there something you'd rather bring? I can do the potato salad."

Darvi quickly recovered her composure. "No, don't be silly. Potato salad it is. I'll see you at noon." She glanced at the clock as she hung up the phone. If she was going to make potato salad for a dozen people, she needed to go to the grocery store immediately.

* * *

At noon Amy, Frank and Bobby stopped by to pick up Darvi and the four of them drove to the park. Darvi scanned the softball field, noting several players tossing the ball and participating in batting practice. She recognized most of them, even though she had never actually been introduced to many of them.

Then Darvi spotted Rance's red sports car pulling into the parking lot on the other side of the diamond. She watched as he extracted his tall frame from the car, walked around to the passenger side, opened the door and stood aside as a very young and very pretty blonde stepped out. Several men on the field called to Rance and he waved a friendly greeting.

Amy's face became animated when she saw them. "There's Rance and Staci. They'll be joining us for lunch after the game." Amy turned toward Darvi as a bit of information she assumed Darvi would find interesting came to mind. "Rance is the one who organizes the softball games. He's been doing it for ten years now."

Darvi answered absently. "That's nice." She eyed Staci. *She can't be over nineteen at most. What's he doing with someone that young?* Darvi continued to watch, only vaguely aware of her irritation. *Well, everyone seems to know her. I guess he must date her regularly. What could they possibly have in common? Humph! Now, that's a pretty stupid question. They probably spend all their time in bed.*

Darvi's thoughts shocked her, and she felt a flush come to her cheeks. She noticed Bobby staring at Staci like a lovesick puppy. *Bobby should be dating her, not Rance. Well, it's none of my business if he dates a mere child.* Again she felt a twinge of guilt at her sarcasm. After all, what possible difference could his dating habits make to her? In spite of the kiss, their relationship was strictly business.

The game started with a flourish, distracting Darvi from her thoughts. Everyone enjoyed a grand time—the onlookers in the bleachers cheered their team; the players were obviously having great fun. Rance played first base. Darvi carefully scrutinized him. He wore jean cutoffs and a tank top. His legs were long, well muscled and very tanned. She recalled his saying he had just returned from Hawaii. The tank top accentuated his broad shoulders, strong arms and muscular chest. A wisp of blond chest hair curled above the tank top. She silently acknowledged the tingle of excitement she felt at the sight of his physique.

She looked to the other side of the bleachers at the young woman who had accompanied Rance. She, too, was quite tanned. Darvi felt the tension building in her body as she wondered if they had shared the two weeks in Hawaii. She refused to believe she might be jealous.

The game ended triumphantly for the home team. They won handily, with Rance clearly the outstanding player. He hit two home runs and executed a crowd-pleasing play at first base.

Darvi felt her stomach knot as she watched Staci run out of the stands, throw her arms around Rance and give him a big hug as he came off the field. They hurried toward the picnic table where Amy and Darvi were now setting out food, Frank and Bobby close on their heels.

"Amy, love, everything looks great. I'm starved." Frank reached for an olive and a couple of carrot sticks as he turned toward Rance. "Hey, buddy. Where's the beer?"

"The cooler's in my car. I'll get it."

"Need any help?"

"I can handle it. Be right back." Rance loped across the softball field to retrieve the drinks.

Amy held her hand out to Staci, who stood alone at the other end of the long table. "Staci, dear, come here and meet Darvi."

Staci smiled and walked over. Up close, Darvi could see Staci's perfect features and big blue eyes. Her tanned skin perfectly complemented her long blond hair. She was indeed very young, even younger than Darvi had first thought—eighteen at the most. Darvi also noted that everyone seemed to know Staci and like her. Bobby could not keep his eyes off her.

"Darvi Stanton, this is Staci Galbraith. Staci lives up in Portland. Darvi is new to our community—she moved here a month ago. She's working with Rance on the renovation of the inn."

Darvi held out her hand and smiled her best professional smile. "It's a pleasure to meet you, Staci. I must tell you, that's a lovely tan you have. Surely you didn't acquire that in Portland at this time of year."

Staci shook Darvi's hand as she replied with the unbridled enthusiasm of youth, "In Portland? Not a chance. We just got back from Hawaii. We were there for two weeks. It was the greatest. Have you ever been there? It was my first time."

Darvi hung on Staci's every word. *We* just got back? *So, Rance had taken her to Hawaii with him.* "Yes, I've been there twice. It's a great place to kick back, relax and soak up the sun."

"Hey!" Rance's shout grabbed everyone's attention. "This thing is heavy. Someone give me a hand." Bobby ran over to him and grasped one handle of the large cooler and the two men carried it back to the table, where they set it down with a thud.

Frank opened the lid and pulled out two cans of beer, tossing one to Rance. The two men immediately pulled the tabs on the cans, took swigs of the cold liquid, set the cans on the table, licked their lips and—in unison—said, "Ahh." Both men laughed.

Amy, Staci and Bobby laughed with them, while Darvi looked slightly perplexed. Amy turned to Darvi and, between giggles, managed to say, "It's their silly postgame ritual. They go through that exact procedure win or lose." Amy whispered conspiratorially in Darvi's ear, "I think it's one of those male bonding things."

Frank quickly spoke up. "Hey, love, we don't make fun of all those silly little female things."

"That, my darling husband, is because we don't have any silly little female rituals." Amy gave her husband a quick, but loving, kiss on his cheek as he patted her affectionately on her bottom. It was so obvious they were a devoted couple, comfortable and secure with each other and their marriage. Both longing and envy darted through Darvi as she watched their closeness.

Rance noted the expression on Darvi's face, then captured her attention with a questioning look. She glanced away, embarrassed at being caught with her feelings showing, if only for a fleeting moment.

"Is it food yet? I'm starved!" The voice belonged to Jim, the third baseman. He called from the field as he and his wife, Elaine, walked toward the picnic table. "I could eat my weight in whatever it is we're having."

Darvi glanced at the approaching couple, and noticed Jim's stomach hanging over the waist of his jeans.

With a quick look at Elaine, Amy patted Jim on the belly. "It appears you already have."

Elaine joined in the good-natured kidding. "And that was just breakfast!" As they laughed with Jim, two other couples arrived at the picnic table.

Everyone eagerly dug into the food, filling their paper plates, and Rance distributed beer and soft drinks. Darvi noticed Staci sneaking her hand into the cooler and withdrawing a can of beer while Rance's attention was busy elsewhere. Without even looking in her direction, he took the can of beer from her and handed her a soft drink.

Staci pouted a moment, then mumbled, "I'm old enough to make up my own mind about what I want to drink."

"Not when you're with me, young lady. When you're old enough to buy it in the store, then you're old enough to drink it." Rance placed the confiscated can of beer back in the cooler and gave Staci a stern look as he closed the lid. She casually shrugged, took her soft drink and sat down next to Bobby.

The women listened as the men replayed every inning of the game, the more spectacular plays two and three times each. Everyone was in high spirits—laughing, eating and generally enjoying a carefree sunny afternoon.

Darvi found the open friendliness of the people very comfortable. They all made her feel welcome, a part of the group. She was actually having a good time and was glad she had accepted Amy's invitation.

Late afternoon brought a cool breeze off the ocean. The unusually sunny, warm day was quickly slipping toward evening. Staci nervously looked at her watch. Finally she walked over to Rance. "I need to get back to my car and start for Portland. It's getting late. Would you drive me?"

Darvi noted the quick knowing look that passed between Amy and Frank and the even quicker one between Frank and Rance.

Frank began gathering his things. "We can drive you to your car, Staci. We have some errands to run and it's right on our way." Then he turned to Rance. "Rance, old buddy, you wouldn't mind collecting all this stuff and dropping it by our place, would you?" He paused as he tried to sound casual. "And give Darvi a lift home?"

"No problem. Glad to do it." Rance turned to Staci. "Now, you drive carefully. I'll see you later." He leaned over, gave her a kiss on the cheek and watched as she trotted off with Bobby to Amy and Frank's car.

When Staci reached the car she waved, then shouted, "Goodbye, Uncle Rance."

"Goodbye, Staci." He returned Staci's wave, doing his best to avoid what he knew would be Darvi's reaction to this bit of news.

"*Uncle* Rance? She's your niece?" Darvi could not hide her astonishment.

Rance adopted an expression of mild irritation and spoke slowly, carefully choosing his words. "Why, of course she's my niece, my older sister's daughter. The whole family spent two weeks in Hawaii together. We

rented a large condo right on the beach.'' He gave her
a stern look. ''Who in the world did you think she
was?'' He waited a moment, more for dramatic effect
than anything else, then continued, ''She's only
seventeen. Surely you couldn't have thought I'd be
dating someone so young. What kind of a man do you
think I am? Some sort of cradle robber?''

Darvi felt her face turning a hot crimson as Rance
leveled a cool blue-eyed gaze directly at her. She tried
to speak. ''Why, I... I mean, I didn't... actually, I
wasn't...'' Finally she just gave up trying to talk at all.
She was only making the situation worse. She did not
know whether to be mad or embarrassed. *He did that
to me on purpose—baiting me, teasing me, trying to
make me jealous.* What upset her the most was that he
had succeeded, she had been jealous. That realization
did not sit comfortably with her.

Suddenly another thought struck her. Amy and
Frank had been in on this from the beginning—right
down to the part where they drove Staci back to her
car, leaving Darvi alone with Rance without any other
transportation. She glared at him. ''You seem to have
arranged this quite nicely. What's supposed to happen now?''

Rance's expression of feigned innocence said his
integrity had been wounded to the core. ''I don't know
what you mean.'' He held her gaze a moment longer.
''What I suggest is that we clean up this mess.'' He
turned to the task at hand, gathering food containers
and clearing the picnic area. He glanced at Darvi,
cocked his head, raised an eyebrow and gave her a
hard look. ''You prefer to watch me work rather than
help?''

Darvi grabbed some dishes and shoved them into a picnic basket as she muttered, "I give up—you're totally impossible."

Wisely, Rance chose not to respond to her comment. Amy had been only too anxious to help him with his little scheme. She had been trying to fix Rance up for so many years she was easy to convince. Frank was another matter. Rance had to threaten to quit the softball team to get Frank's cooperation. Not that Frank had anything against Darvi. He just kept saying that Rance was the last of the truly carefree bachelors and he did not want to see him forced into domestic servitude. That comment caused Amy to threaten to make Frank's life miserable, and she had even hinted at curtailing certain bedroom activities. It had done the trick.

Rance felt a little guilty about using Staci that way. But he would never have thought of it if she had not called early that morning to say she was driving down to watch their game. Reading between the lines, he knew she did not care at all about the softball game—she wanted to see Bobby. So, as long as she was in town...

Darvi finished packing away the leftover food and the dishes, while he gathered all the trash and disposed of it. When each was satisfied the picnic area was clean, Rance picked up the large cooler and Darvi grabbed the picnic basket.

Before long, the red sports car was moving down a side street, passing neat, well-cared-for older homes. Rance pulled into the driveway of Amy and Frank's house. "Sit tight. I'll just take their things around to the back and leave them in the kitchen."

Darvi watched as he walked effortlessly across the lawn and around the corner of the house. His body movements were strong but graceful. She found herself retaining an image of his retreating form even after he had rounded the corner and disappeared from sight. A nervous shiver shook her as she sat in the car, waiting for him to return.

Her mind drifted back three years, to the first time Jerry Peterson had walked into her Laguna Beach studio. His black curly hair and piercing dark eyes had immediately captured her attention. They had started seeing each other casually—lunch now and then, a drink at the end of the work day, an occasional afternoon at a new gallery showing or a movie.

Their relationship had grown closer, until finally they had become lovers. Darvi knew, in retrospect, that she should have seen what was happening. Whenever she tried to discuss their future, he skillfully changed the subject. He put her off with pretty words and flowery phrases; he gave her answers that really did not have any substance. She should have suspected something was amiss, but she was so enamored by the attention he showered on her that she ignored her nagging fears.

Having a lover was something new to Darvi. She had never before experienced the type of lovemaking Jerry had introduced to their relationship. She was a virtual novice—not a virgin, just inexperienced—when their affair had begun. He had been an effective teacher, but she now realized that most of their lovemaking had been for his pleasure, not their mutual enjoyment. Then that horrible night...

The gentle caress against her cheek came from the open car window. It was followed by the smooth masculine voice that startled Darvi out of her thoughts.

"Where were you just now? The look on your face placed you a million miles from here, lost in some sort of private purgatory." Rance stood next to the car, leaning against the passenger door. He studied her face for a long moment, looked searchingly into her emerald eyes. "I am a good listener, Darvi."

Four

<hr />

Darvi returned his look. Gone was the arrogance and the adversarial challenge that he seemed to wear like a badge. In their stead was an open sincerity and concern. Another shiver shook her. She wanted to be able to tell someone, to unburden herself, but she knew she would never be able to. Her secret was so terrible she did not dare trust anyone. Suddenly her fears kicked in and she shut down her emotions, once again closing the door. This time, however, she did not conceal everything with anger.

Rance saw the emotional turmoil as he gazed into her eyes. He saw an anxiety, almost a pleading for understanding, flicker across her face. Then he saw her bury the feelings and put on the mask she so expertly wore.

Her voice was almost childlike as she said, "I'm fine." Then she added, so softly as to be almost inaudible, "Thank you. Maybe sometime..." Her voice trailed off and she did not finish her sentence.

He tucked back a loose tendril of her copper-colored hair, then cupped her chin with his hand, raising her face until he could look into her eyes. "What could possibly have happened to hurt you so deeply you would choose to close yourself off from the world?"

His question went unanswered.

Rance withdrew his hand and walked around the car to the driver's side and slid in behind the wheel. "I'd better get you home. The breeze is turning cooler." He allowed his eyes to peruse her long bare legs, the shorts she was wearing and the outline of her firm breasts beneath her T-shirt. "Besides, you're not exactly dressed for warmth."

Darvi managed a shy smile as she again took in his tanned, muscular body. "Neither are you."

When they reached her place he walked with her to the door of her studio rather than just dropping her off at the curb. As she inserted the key into the lock he quickly covered her hand with his. "Here, let me do that."

He had expected her to yank her hand away at his touch. He was pleasantly surprised when she let her hand linger before she slowly withdrew it. He unlocked the door and looked inside the room. Once he saw that everything was okay, he stepped aside. He followed her through the door, closing it behind him.

She had not intended to let Rance come in, especially after the dirty trick he had pulled on her that afternoon. The truth was, though, she had been pleased he had gone to all that trouble just to be able to drive her home. She even forgave Amy and Frank for their part in the deception.

Before she lost her nerve Darvi whirled around and faced him, offering a tentative smile. "Would you like some coffee or tea? It won't take but a moment for me to fix some."

The surprise in his eyes gave way to pleasure as he answered, "I'd like that very much. Coffee, if that's okay."

"Coffee it is. Make yourself comfortable. I'll be right back." She hurried toward the small kitchen as he watched her with an excited intensity until she disappeared from sight.

Rance casually picked up sketches from her work table, studied them briefly, then replaced them. He slowly made his way to the small sitting area toward the back of the studio, carefully avoiding her bedroom door.

Darvi busied herself in the kitchen, making coffee, gathering cups and finding a serving tray. She tried not to dwell on the fact that she had let down her guard, allowed Rance into her personal domain for a non-business purpose, had even been the one to suggest he stay for coffee. She knew that if she stopped to consider her actions she would ask Rance to leave, would remove all temptation.

She paused for a moment, her brow furrowed in concentration. Panic stabbed through her as she looked toward where he sat on her couch. Temptation is exactly what he was—an overwhelming temptation to which she must not succumb.

She glanced down at her hands and was surprised to see them trembling. Her eyes misted as she fought back the tears. *I can't become involved with him. I could never tell him about what happened. He would never understand...*

The loud crash startled Rance. He bolted toward the noise, then stopped dead in his tracks at the kitchen door. Darvi stood in the middle of the room, a tray and broken coffee cups at her feet. He saw the look of pain on her face, the fear in her eyes, as the tears rolled down her cheeks. Her entire body trembled as if she were cold.

He hesitated for a moment, not sure what to do. She looked so in need of comfort. The need touched what he had thought was a carefully buried place inside him. He walked over and put his arms around her, drawing her to him. He placed his hand gently at the back of her head and rested it against his shoulder. He felt her shiver as he held her.

After a long, silent moment she tentatively reached her arms around him and held on, gaining comfort from his strength and closeness. A few moments later she started to pull back, to extricate herself from his arms. She was not sure how she had allowed herself to become enfolded in his embrace, but she did know it was not going to happen again.

As she struggled he tightened his hold on her. "No, you don't. You're not going to run away."

Her voice quavered as she fought back more tears. She tried her best to project her shell of toughness. With clenched fists she pushed harder against his taut chest. "How dare you try to hold me here against my will. How many times do I need to tell you that nothing's wrong? I'm fine."

His eyes narrowed as his look pierced through to her core. His voice was carefully controlled, yet projected his total control of the situation. "I guess you'll just have to keep telling me until I believe it." A hint of sarcasm crept into his tone. "At the rate we're going, that could take years.'' He moved his hand up her back to the copper-colored French braid, then worked at releasing the clasp that held it together.

He felt her muscles relax as some of the tension drained from her body. He combed his fingers through her long thick hair as the braid unraveled and the tresses fell around her shoulders. "Come on, let's go in the other room.'' He edged her toward the kitchen door.

"No, wait.'' She frantically searched for something, anything, to change a mood that was rapidly becoming intimate. "I…'' Her gaze continued to dart around the kitchen, then lit on the broken cups on the floor. "I have to clean up this mess.''

"It'll still be here later. Come on.'' Rance gently, but firmly, escorted her out of the kitchen and to the couch. He turned her face toward him, again looked deeply into her frightened eyes for a long moment, then said, "Now, start at the beginning. Tell me what happened.''

She actually felt protected, cared for and comforted. It was a strange feeling, one she had not experienced in a long time. However, she was sure that giving in to that feeling, permitting him into her life, would only end with more pain, hurt and emotional upheaval.

Tears welled in her eyes as images from the past flashed through her mind. Her body started to tremble again. Her thoughts screamed at her, creating a deafening roar in her head. *How can I tell him? The doctor said it wasn't my fault, I shouldn't blame myself. He was wrong. The psychologist said it wasn't my fault. She was wrong, too. They were both wrong. How can I tell Rance the truth—that I was responsi-*

ble for the death of my baby! The tears slipped down her cheeks as she tried to control her rising panic.

Darvi was not the only one experiencing panic. Rance found himself in the unaccustomed position of offering emotional support and comfort. It had been years since he had extended himself this way and it caused him tremors of anxiety. He tentatively pressed her head to his shoulder as he stroked her hair, his voice tender as he talked to her. "Whatever this is, you can't continue to carry it around with you."

She spoke haltingly, reluctant to continue. "You've been pushing me ever since we met. I don't think we should—"

He felt her tense as she started to push away from his embrace.

"Okay. We don't need to talk right now. We'll just sit here for a little while and get comfortable with each other." He held her tightly, but not so tight that she felt she was being held against her will.

A calm settled over Darvi. Rance's touch and soft words soothed her as she nestled in his arms. He was really very nice when he wanted to be—gentle, caring, considerate. And he was incredibly sexy. Her eyelids grew heavy as the turmoil took its toll. She felt herself drift toward sleep, her last conscious thought whether she could really trust this man—trust him not to turn against her or abandon her if she told him the truth. She had a vague impression of Rance shifting his weight slightly as he moved her into a more comfortable position, then darkness prevailed.

He watched as she slept peacefully in his arms. Her long copper tresses framed her beautiful face and fanned out over her shoulders. She was truly lovely. He wondered again why she had left Southern California to settle in the small coastal town of Sandy Cove, Oregon. It was almost as if she had run away from something. Although he could not explain it, did not understand why it should be so, for some reason he felt he had to help her exorcise whatever demons haunted her.

He continued to hold her while she slept. His body ached from his uncomfortable position, but he dared not move for fear of disturbing her. Without warning, her breathing became labored and her peaceful features contorted in anguish. She thrashed about, turning her head from side to side as if trying to ward off some terrible evil. She mumbled something, but Rance could not quite make it out. Her agitation increased.

He pulled her tightly against him, rocking her in his arms. He forced a calm to his voice, not sure exactly what was happening or whether she could actually hear him. "Darvi, it's okay. Don't worry." He stroked her hair as he continued to hold her.

Darvi's face softened. Her breathing returned to normal. She appeared to be responding to his words. Whatever it was that had invaded her sleep seemed to have gone. He seriously questioned whether he was taking on more than he was prepared to handle. He studied the way she nestled in his arms. A warm feeling spread through him as he allowed his own deeply buried feelings to surface. Someone *needed* him—*she* needed him. It had been more years than he could remember since anyone had needed him. He furrowed his brow in concentration, once again not at all sure he was doing the right thing.

The sun dropped from sight and darkness pervaded the studio. The only illumination was the bright moonlight filtering through the window. Darvi stirred, and he immediately tightened his loose hold on her.

She shook the grogginess from her head as she opened her eyes and tried to focus in the darkness. She was momentarily confused about where she was and what had happened. Then everything came back to her in a flash.

"What time is it?" A wariness crept into her voice. "How long have I been sleeping? Why is it so dark in here?"

"In order—it's eight o'clock, about an hour and a half, and I didn't want to disturb you by getting up to turn on a light." He brushed her hair from her cheek as he allowed a moment's serious reflection. "I like your hair down like this."

Her first reaction involved panic, she wanted to get some distance between her and this very tempting man. For reasons unknown even to Darvi, however, she did not move. She stayed on the couch next to him and said haltingly, "I don't wear my hair down because it gets in my way when I work. Once I actually sealed the ends into a window I was doing. I finally had to cut the ends off to get my hair free." She looked around the darkened room. "I think we should turn on some lights."

He eased her away from him, then stood up and stretched his aching muscles. He snapped on a table lamp and looked around. "It's getting chilly in here. Where's the thermostat?"

"In the hall." Darvi shivered as the chill in the air hit her bare arms and legs. She had not realized how cold it was, she had felt so warm and protected in Rance's arms. "If you'll excuse me for a minute, I'll be right back.'' She hurried to her bedroom, sliding the door shut behind her.

She sank onto the bed, her mind reeling. *What have I gotten myself into?* Her uncertainty and confusion were playing havoc with her logic. She rose and removed her shorts and T-shirt, then grabbed an old pair of jeans and a warm sweatshirt, dressing quickly. Finally, she pulled on a pair of warm socks. Her mind worked overtime as she attempted to sort out conflicting thoughts. She knew Rance had been correct. She could not continue to run away from life, she had to face up to her fears. Just because her relationship with Jerry Peterson ended in an agonizingly painful manner did not mean that another relationship would follow the same course. She allowed herself a slight bittersweet laugh—besides, she was now older, and certainly much wiser.

She remembered Rance's kiss on the patio of the art gallery. He had called the situation correctly. She had wanted him to kiss her, then she had become frightened. She had known at that very moment how much she was attracted to him and it had scared her to death.

Darvi took a deep, steadying breath. She would give this relationship with Rance a fair try. It could not be as painful as what she had already been through. It could not hurt as much as Jerry Peterson's betrayal of her trust and what she had thought at that time was love. Nothing could hurt her as much as the loss of her baby. She opened the bedroom door and returned to the kitchen.

Rance was standing in front of the open refrigerator door, staring at the contents. Finally he reached for an opened bottle of white wine and poured himself a glass. He had already cleaned up the broken coffee cups.

"You could pour me one of those, too, if you don't mind," she said determinedly. Her eyes drifted over his taut chest, broad shoulders and muscular arms and legs. He was indeed a sexy and desirable man. It had been a long time since she had allowed herself to desire a sexy man. She could no longer bury such desires. *Maybe he'll be able to...I hope he can understand about...*

She shook her head to stop the thoughts. She knew at that moment that she wanted to tell him about Jerry Peterson, about the baby—about everything. She also knew she would not tell him for a while, until she felt more comfortable with him and the situation—more confident that he was not really the arrogant jerk he usually presented himself as. Trust was a difficult thing for her, it no longer came easy. She wanted to trust him; she would try.

Rance stared at her, taking in every nuance of her being. She had run a brush through her hair. The long copper tresses flowed around her shoulders. Something about her—perhaps the look in her eyes—was somehow different. She appeared calmer, more relaxed. He sensed a new vulnerability, an openness— and he felt panicky.

He reached for another wineglass. He was not sure exactly how to treat the situation. His manner stiffened and he heard an edge creep into his voice as he pointed to the floor. "I cleaned up your mess for you." He poured a second glass of wine and handed it to her. He saw the flush that momentarily highlighted her cheeks.

Darvi caught the uncertainty in Rance's eyes as he handed her one of the wineglasses. She was not sure how to respond to his change in attitude. She hesitated for a moment before speaking. "I'm sorry about—"

But he cut her off in midsentence. "Come on." He grabbed her hand. "Let's sit down and talk." He led her back to the couch and sat next to her. He was treading on totally unfamiliar ground, putting himself into a realm that called for sharing, patience and understanding.

She nervously played with her glass. Finally she asked, "What do you want to talk about?"

"I want to talk about you." Again he heard a cool, almost analytical, tone in his voice—not at all the tone of voice to elicit confidence from someone. He struggled with his own conflicts as he watched her nervousness.

She took a deep breath to try to calm her jitters. Finally she started to speak, not really sure if she was angry with him and his less-than-cordial attitude or simply uncomfortable with the topic. Either way, her words were cloaked in defensiveness. "I had my life under control until I ran into you. I'm not a helpless little thing who cries at the drop of a hat. I've always been able to take care of myself, handle any situation that came along. You're asking too much too fast." The tears welled in her eyes as her facade began to crumble. "I can't really talk about it, not all of it, not yet. Please don't push me so hard. It's very difficult for me . . . very painful."

It was the arrogant Rance who started to speak, the words sounding harsh. "Pushing you? I haven't—" But the rest of the sentence stuck in his throat. His involuntary reaction to her spoken words and unspoken fears was to pull her into his embrace. He stroked her hair as he thought over what she had said. He had not realized he had been pushing her that hard or that her secret was so painful. Now he considered it a major concession on her part that she had revealed as much as she had. He would back off and give her room. She would tell him what she could when she was ready.

The pendulum clock chimed midnight. In spite of an occasional clash of wills during the course of the evening, they had spent almost four hours talking and laughing. Darvi was a different person than Rance had previously experienced. She was open, as long as the conversation was not too personal. She was witty, charming...a joy to be with. He asked himself several times how this delightful woman could have hidden behind all that anger.

He glanced at the clock as it sounded the hour. "I can't believe it's this late." He eyed her longingly for a brief moment, then returned his attention to reality. "I'd better leave and let you get some sleep." They walked to the front door together. "Besides, if I don't get my car out from in front of your place, the local gossips will have us as an item before breakfast is over."

His gaze lingered on her mouth as he leaned against the front door. He took her face in his hands and held it for a moment before lowering his head. His lips brushed hers, then he captured her parted lips, drinking in her tantalizing sweetness.

He captured her mouth, drinking in the taste that was uniquely hers. He reveled in the softness of her

lips, the texture of her mouth, the excitement of her
tongue touching his. Her breathing quickened to
match his own, the firmness of her full breasts pressed
against his chest, her hands gently stroked the length
of his back. He marveled at her sensuality. He felt his
passions being drawn into an uncontrollable vortex.
He knew they must stop before it was too late.

Rance's kiss was exquisite. Darvi melted into his
arms as he embraced her being. She allowed his mouth
to envelope her—his lips nibbling, teasing, devour-
ing. His tongue probed the darkness of her mouth,
searching and exploring. He made her feel things she
thought she would never feel again, longings she
thought had been buried never to be resurrected.

Darvi experienced the pull of Rance's passion. In a
flash she knew making love with him would be unlike
anything she had ever before experienced—ever
imagined, even in her wildest flights of fantasy. She
also knew they must stop before it was too late, before they gave in to the desire rapidly building between them.

She pulled back from his embrace, and saw the
smoky-blue passion in his eyes as he caressed her
cheek with his fingertips. She had trouble finding her
voice. Finally she spoke, breathless as she tried to for-
mulate her words. "I...I think you'd better—" he
brushed his lips against hers again, sending tingling
sensations through her body "—leave before it gets
any later." He again captured her mouth with a force
that left her weak in the knees and almost limp in his
arms.

He felt her tremble as she pressed her body against
his. "Yes, I think you're right."

Reluctantly, he released her. He never let his guard down with women. He preferred to keep things casual. With Darvi, he found himself letting it down once again. He held her face tenderly in his hands as he looked searchingly into her eyes. "You're someone special, Darvi Stanton. Don't ever sell yourself short."

"Thank you, Rance. Thank you for wanting to understand."

His muscles tensed. A stern look crossed his face as his entire persona seemed to change right before her eyes. His voice had lost the soft edge that had been there just moments earlier. "We're not through talking about this. Don't think you can get away with working your wiles on me like that."

His words shocked her, especially coming immediately after the passionate kisses they had just shared. She retreated behind her wall, her voice angry. "Me? I'm not the one who initiated the kiss—"

"I'd really better get out of here." He opened the door, ran quickly through the cold night air, climbed in his car and drove down the dark street.

She leaned against the front door as she shut it, closed her eyes and put her fingertips to her lips. She did not understand what had just happened. Everything had been going so well. Then all of a sudden Rance seemed to transform from the tender, caring and sensual man who had been with her the prior four hours into the arrogant, insensitive jerk she had encountered the day they had met.

She walked to her bedroom, quickly undressed and climbed into bed, pulling the down comforter up to her chin. She closed her eyes. The confusion swirled through her mind. What had she done to cause such a drastic change in his demeanor? She recalled the passion of his kisses, his tender touch. She simply did not know what to make of him and his mood changes. She finally fell asleep, but it was not a peaceful sleep.

Rance pulled his car into the garage. He sat behind the wheel for a long time, his brow furrowed as he berated himself for the manner in which he had left Darvi's studio. She had not deserved such brusqueness. He was not quite sure exactly what prompted him to behave that way. There was something about her that touched him and it scared him to death.

He tried to put some rational thought to what had happened that evening, how much of himself he had exposed and why—what he had opened himself up to by trying to dig into her past. Once again he realized he was not at all sure how to handle the situation. How hard should he push her? Should he back off and let her have her own time frame?

This was the first time since his disastrous marriage and divorce that he had wanted to know anything about the person inside rather than just the physical woman. His uneasiness over the situation made him question his motives. Was it a genuine desire to help her with whatever was troubling her or was it just curiosity about her apparently troubled past?

Finally he climbed out of the car, but did not go into his house. Instead, he headed out back to his workshop. Keeping busy would be good therapy. It would take his mind off Darvi.

Five

Darvi lay in bed as the morning sun streamed through the window. She stretched out her long legs, wiggled her toes and rolled over onto her stomach. It was going to be another unusually sunny, warm day.

Her mind drifted to thoughts of Rance Coulter. Last night she had decided to trust Rance. The decision had been made prior to his abrupt departure. Perhaps it had been too impulsive. In the bright light of day, without the distraction of his closeness, she reviewed that decision. He was arrogant, pushy, demanding, even occasionally rude—certainly not qualities she found endearing. But then he would turn around and be tender, caring and understanding. Which was the real Rance? She raised her fingertips to her lips as the remembered sensation of his kiss filled her being. A smile curled the corners of her mouth. Her decision would stand; she would trust him.

She felt a lightness of spirit she had not experienced in several years. She threw back the covers and climbed out of bed. The energy flowed through her; the prospect of a new day excited her. She looked forward to whatever was in store.

Rance opened his eyes and focused on the clock by his bed. It had been almost five in the morning when he had left his workshop and finally gone to sleep. Now it was eleven o'clock. Six hours' sleep was enough. He headed for the shower.

He emerged from his bathroom dripping water across the floor. The hot shower had taken some of the kinks out of his muscles. The first softball game of the season always made him sore. He refused to entertain the idea that he might be sore because he was getting older and did not exercise as much as he used to.

He dressed quickly, then reached for the phone. He waited impatiently as the phone rang—three, four, five rings. Darvi finally answered.

The sound of Rance's voice sent shivers up her spine. A warm blanket of caring settled over her—a feeling of euphoria, a sense of calm well-being.

"Have you had breakfast yet?"

She looked at the clock. "Breakfast? It's almost noon. Did you just get up?"

"Don't be ridiculous. Of course not. Obviously, I meant to say brunch. Have you had brunch yet?"

Her laugh was warm and open. "No, I haven't eaten yet."

"Good! I'll pick you up in fifteen minutes." Before she could say yes or no, he broke the phone connection.

It seemed that everybody in town was enjoying the unseasonably warm, sunny weather. The outside dining patio of the Wine Bistro did not have an empty table. Rance and Darvi made their way through the crowd to a table for six, next to the railing. Amy, Frank, Jim and Elaine were already seated and enjoying their Sunday-brunch champagne.

Frank called out to Rance as he held up his almost empty champagne glass, "As you can see, we waited for you." He glanced at Darvi, his look embarrassed. It was obvious he felt guilty about participating in Rance's scheme following the softball game. Darvi's smile was warm and outgoing, telling Frank she was not angry with him.

Everyone exchanged greetings as Jim filled the two remaining champagne glasses. Rance turned toward Darvi, clinked his glass to hers and took a sip of champagne, his eyes never leaving her face. Darvi flushed as she lowered her eyelids and raised the glass to her lips.

Amy and Frank exchanged a quick, knowing look. Jim and Elaine seemed oblivious to the silent energy that flowed between Darvi and Rance. Brunch moved along happily, with everyone laughing and talking. Jim made two trips to the buffet table. When he rose to make his third, Elaine stopped him.

"Jim, enough is enough."

"But honey, it says 'all you can eat.' I'm still hungry."

Elaine gave an exasperated sigh. "I'll fix you something when we get home." Jim sat down in his chair, a disappointed look on his face.

Amy nudged Frank's leg with her knee, not wanting to draw attention to her actions. She caught his eye, then nodded unobtrusively toward Darvi and

Rance. Frank looked in the direction, then smiled as he turned his gaze back to Amy.

During the course of the meal Rance had casually inched his chair closer and closer to Darvi's. His right hand and her left hand were both hidden under the table as he laced their fingers together in a warm, caring manner.

Finally Jim and Elaine moved to break up their group. Elaine looked at Jim as she slowly shook her head. "I've got to get him home and feed him. He's had only two meals so far today and here it is already two o'clock."

Jim grinned self-consciously. "I have to keep up my strength." He shot a quick, lustful look in Elaine's direction, then turned his attention to the rest of the group. "Who knows, I might even get lucky this afternoon."

Elaine rolled her eyes in mock irritation. Slowly an impish grin crossed her face. "We'd better get out of here while he's still in the mood."

Everyone laughed as Elaine and Jim said their goodbyes and made their way across the patio toward the door.

Amy quickly gathered her purse and stood up. "I hate to abandon you two, but Frank and I have several things to do today and we'd better get started."

Frank looked at his wife in confusion. "What things?" Amy shot him a look that only a husband could understand. "Oh, yeah. Those things." Frank quickly rose to his feet.

The couple departed after a few minutes of idle chitchat. Darvi and Rance were left alone. She sipped the last of her coffee. He watched her closely.

"Would you like some more?"

She pushed the cup and saucer across the table. "No way. I don't know where I'd put it." She looked up at him. His gaze captured her in its spell. Once again he seemed to be exerting some sort of mystical power over her. Gone was the arrogance and in its place were the warmth and caring that made her pulse race with excitement.

"If you're sure you don't want anything else, then I guess we'd better leave." He rose from his seat and held her chair for her as she stepped away from the table.

Rance placed his hand against her back and guided her through the restaurant, out to the parking lot. When they reached his sports car, he wrapped both arms around her and leaned her back against the door. He looked intently into her green eyes for a moment, then lowered his mouth to hers.

Darvi hesitated as their lips brushed. She quickly regained her composure and pulled her head away from his. Her voice was filled with surprise. "What do you think you're doing, right here in the parking lot of a busy restaurant? I thought you were worried about the local tongues."

He lightly drew his fingertips across the smooth skin of her cheek as he continued to encircle her with his other arm. "I think we're too late. Didn't you notice, my pet, how quickly everyone deserted us after we finished eating?"

My pet? Darvi stiffened at the sound of the words. It was what Jerry Peterson had called her.

Rance noticed Darvi's reaction and immediately straightened. "What's wrong?"

She spit out a reply as she attempted to move away from him. "Nothing."

He was equally angry. He quickly grabbed her shoulders and used his body to trap her against the car, preventing her from turning and leaving. "Don't think you can tell me nothing's wrong and get away with it." His searched her face for some answers. "What did I say to upset you? What did I do?"

Darvi glared at him for a minute, then spoke, her voice a mixture of anger and hurt. "I'm not your *pet*, nor am I your plaything."

Guilt stabbed his consciousness as he realized exactly what he had said and how she had interpreted it. It certainly had not been his intention to imply any such thing. He studied her defiant glare. Slowly he wrapped his arms around her again, drawing her to him. At first she offered some resistance, then she folded into his embrace. Rance spoke softly, almost whispering in her ear. "No, you're not." He kissed her tenderly on the cheek. "It was a bad choice of words. I'm sorry." It was quite a concession on his part. Rance Coulter seldom apologized, and certainly not for some innocent comment said without malice.

Her voice was very soft. "I'm sorry, too. I've made a big deal about an innocent statement—again."

He looked intently into her eyes, still searching for answers. "Is that part of what this is about? Someone from your past—some man—who treated you that way?" He embraced her tightly, stroking her hair as he held her head against his shoulder. He sensed her need for care and understanding, not badgering. He continued to talk to her, his words soft and comforting as he held her. "It's going to be okay. We'll work this out." He felt her tremble slightly as he leaned against her.

Rance held her for several minutes, neither of them saying anything. Finally Darvi raised her head and gazed into his honest blue eyes. She offered him a shy smile. "I'm okay now. Really I am."

He leaned down and kissed her tenderly on the lips, then looked into her troubled face, not at all sure how far to push her, especially after her outburst the previous evening. "Who was he? Who was the guy who did this to you?"

She hesitated a moment. She had told herself she would trust this man. Perhaps now was the time. She took a deep breath to calm the butterflies in her stomach. The words came out quietly—almost inaudibly. "His name was Jerry Peterson. I met him one warm sunny afternoon three years ago when he wandered into my studio in Laguna Beach. He was almost twenty years older than I was—charming, captivating, dynamic... and forceful."

Rance jerked to attention. *Forceful? Did this lowlife slime force her—rape her?*

His arms involuntarily tightened around her as he narrowed his eyes in anger. His heart pounded wildly. He tried to keep his voice calm. He did not want Darvi to jump to the wrong conclusion by thinking he was angry with her. "This Jerry Peterson, did he... uh... force you—"

She felt his arms tighten around her, saw the look on his face. She spoke with urgency as she placed her fingers on his lips. "No, that's not what happened—not what you're thinking. There was no coercion."

She stopped talking, rested her head against his shoulder and did not say another word. Several minutes passed in silence as he cradled her in his arms. He was not sure what to do—whether to simply hold her, encourage her to continue talking, or put her in the car and drive her home.

She made the decision for him. She slowly extricated herself from his embrace and peered around the parking lot. "We'd probably better leave before we start drawing a crowd." She looked into his eyes and gave him a tentative smile as she lightly touched his cheek with her fingertips.

He reached up and captured her hand in his. It bothered him that there had been something so traumatic in her life it could be an obstacle between them. He had given it a lot of thought. He wanted to know more about her because he genuinely cared about her. Where all of this might lead still scared him, but he was warming to the possibility of a relationship. "We're going to talk. Where would you like to go, your place or mine?" He saw the uncertainty come into her eyes. She started to say something, but he stopped her. "Before you offer me a multitude of excuses, let me tell you something."

He looked at her, plumbed the depths of her consciousness, as he collected his words. He continued in a calm voice that carried the weight of absolute authority. He was not offering her choices, he was not asking what she wanted. He was telling her what would be. "We're going somewhere right now and we're going to talk this out. Nothing is as bad when you share it in the light of day as when you hide it away in a dark closet."

She returned his look, glanced down at the ground and then back to his face. A sigh of resignation escaped her lips. "You're not going to let this go, are you? You're going to keep after me until you have what you want." Her eyes were searching, questioning and frightened. "What happens, Rance, if I tell you everything you want to know and you find it as horrible as I know it is? What if you aren't able to forgive what happened? Then what?"

The questions caught Rance totally by surprise. This was not what he had expected her to say. He studied her for a long moment. "What could possibly be that terrible?"

"You're asking me to relive the most horrible thing that has ever happened to me, that will ever happen to me. You're asking me to bring it out in the open—all the pain and hurt. And you're expecting me to do this on blind faith, just because you say *trust me.*" Darvi's voice took on a hard, bitter edge. Her eyes narrowed as they grew distant and angry. "Believe me, I've heard *trust me* before. I've heard it said with all the sincerity and caring that are possible to inject into those two words."

He did not back down. He firmly stood his ground, refusing to give her the space he knew she was hoping for. "You're already doing it to yourself. You live it over and over again every day."

Darvi felt herself being drawn into the honesty she saw in Rance's eyes. Everything he said to her made sense—logically. But emotionally, none of it did. She felt as if she were being torn apart, as if a great civil war was being waged and she was the battleground.

He saw the tears well in her eyes, the confusion and uncertainty on her face. She squeezed her eyelids tightly shut, her face contorted in anguish. She tried to speak, but words would not come out.

She tried again. She forced the words out, her voice small and frightened. "I want to trust you, Rance. Really I do. But...it's just that..." She opened her eyes, held his look for a moment, then lowered her gaze. "Can we please go? Would you take me home?"

"Of course I'll drive you home."

Rance walked Darvi to her front door, took her key from her hand and inserted it into the lock. He swung the door open and stepped aside so she could enter the studio. She immediately turned to face him, blocking his way. "Thank you for brunch."

He grabbed her around the waist, lifted her off the floor and set her to one side. She stood in stunned silence as he came in, too, closed the door and turned to face her. He took her hands in his and led her to the couch, seating her in the corner. He stared into her eyes, watching her shifting emotions as she wrestled with the dilemma.

Darvi nervously clasped and unclasped her hands, twirled an errant strand of hair, then took a steadying breath. Her gaze darted around the room, before it returned to Rance. He put his arm around her shoulder, sharing his strength and giving her support.

She closed her eyes, afraid to look at him. Her heart pounded with anxiety. But slowly the words came out. "Like I said, he was dynamic, forceful. I'd never met anyone like him. My experience with men was limited, I didn't date much. He just sort of swept me off my feet. It was easy for him—flowers, lots of compliments, pretty words. He buried me in attention and flattery. No one had ever treated me like that before, paid that kind of attention to me."

She stopped talking for a moment, taking another steadying breath before continuing. She silently pleaded for his understanding. "Can you comprehend how that could happen? I was just so overwhelmed by all the attention and flattery.

"At first we saw each other casually, once or twice a week. We would have lunch, sometimes attend a gallery showing, occasionally go to a movie. This went on for a little over a month. He would call me almost every day whether we saw each other or not. He began to make his intentions clear, the direction he wanted our relationship to take. He planned our future—" she paused as a sob caught in her throat. "Or at least that's what I thought he was doing."

He saw a single tear slip silently down her cheek. He kissed her forehead and held her closer. After taking a deep breath, she continued.

"He became jealous of my time and my friends. Soon, with the exception of my work, he had me isolated from almost everything that had been part of my life before we met. It all happened so smoothly I didn't realize what was going on. Some of my friends tried to warn me about him, but I wouldn't listen. I rationalized everything by telling myself that anyone who was as attentive and giving as he was couldn't be bad for me."

She turned toward Rance, her eyes filled with pain. "Only he wasn't a giving, loving man. He was selfish and cruel. Not cruel as in physically abusive. He was psychologically cruel. He tried to make me feel guilty whenever I didn't comply with something he wanted. He would give me a hurt look and say things like 'I thought you loved me.' To this day, I don't fully understand how I allowed it to happen." Her voice became loud and forceful. "I don't know why I just didn't tell him to go to hell."

She paused to reconsider what she had just said. Then her voice again turned soft. "I guess I thought I was in love with him and he was in love with me. It was my obligation, my duty, to please him, to make him happy. The more I did, the more he demanded. We had been lovers for almost a year when my world fell apart."

She reached for Rance's hand, grasping it tightly as she sought out his strength. "I simply couldn't believe I was pregnant. The first time we'd made love Jerry told me not to worry about it. I assumed he meant he had a vasectomy. I wasn't secure enough, self-confident enough to demand he explain exactly what he meant by that. I should have taken steps immediately to protect myself, but, foolishly, I didn't. I trusted what he said. It was a miracle that a year passed without my becoming pregnant."

Rance's heart ached as he listened to her story, the pain in her eyes almost more than he could handle. It had never occurred to him that her turmoil would be so deep-seated.

"I went to the doctor. I didn't tell Jerry about the appointment. The tests confirmed that I was pregnant. It was a week after that before I saw Jerry. He had been out of town on business."

She shifted her weight slightly, still holding tightly to Rance's hand. Her fingernails dug into his skin. "The evening he returned we were at my studio. It had been raining for three days, one of those ongoing Southern California winter storms. He saw how nervous and upset I was and asked what was wrong. He apparently thought the storm was bothering me. I didn't know the proper procedure for telling a lover I was pregnant." She took a steadying breath before continuing with what she knew was the most painful part of her story.

"In my mind, I saw him throwing his arms around me and telling me how much he loved me—how thrilled he was about the baby. He'd ask me to marry him and we'd live happily ever after." Her voice became almost a whisper. "I soon found out that was a fairy tale meant only for little girls to believe in."

Darvi had been using every ounce of strength she could muster to hold back the storm that threatened to burst forth from her inner turmoil. She started to shiver, the shivers quickly turning into violent tremors as the pent-up emotions refused to be contained any longer. She knew she had to tell him the rest while she was still able.

Rance continued to hold her, but his embrace was mechanical more than purposeful. He felt numb inside. Her story touched more than his compassion; it exacerbated his own pain and conflicts. He knew the story so well, but he knew it from his perspective. It was the ploy Joan had used to get him to marry her: she had told him she was pregnant. Even though he did not love her, he had done the honorable thing and married her. It did not take long for him to discover she had lied to him. When he had confronted her she had given him a coy smile, batted her long eyelashes and told him she hoped he was not too angry with her for her little *deception*.

He had done his best to make the marriage work. All his efforts were wasted, however, when seven months later Joan ran off with a former boyfriend. Rance vowed at that time that he would never again allow himself to get so close to a women that he would become emotionally involved. He had since restricted himself to the fun and games. If it looked like things were turning serious he would break it off. He had not once allowed himself to be drawn into a relationship or an emotional commitment during the past ten years.

Yet here he was, actually encouraging an emotional situation with a woman who made him feel things he did not want to feel. His inner being told him to escape while he could still get out. His basic decent instincts, however, told him that he had pushed her into this confession and it was his obligation to stick with her through the ensuing upheaval it had caused. He forced his attention away from his own bothersome thoughts and returned it to what Darvi was saying.

The tears flowed freely from her eyes and streamed down her cheeks. She spoke through her sobs. "I told him straight out I was pregnant. He just stared at me, then let out a cruel chuckle. The expression on his face was so cold—so uncaring. Then he looked at me and said, 'What do you expect me to do about it? You should have been more careful.' I'll never forget those words."

She could not say any more as the sobs wracked her body. He cradled her head against his shoulder and rocked her gently in his arms. He clenched his jaw in anger as he replayed her words in his mind. He was not exactly sure about the source of his anger—whether it was his own bitter memories of a woman claiming she was pregnant and he was the father, or if it was because some man had turned Darvi's life into a living nightmare. He continued to hold her and gently rock her as her sobs began to subside. She started to pull away from him and sit up straight so that she could compose herself and continue talking.

Rance kissed her on the cheek, tasting the saltiness of her tears. His being ached, he felt her pain. His voice was warm and caring. "You don't need to say anything more right now. We can talk later, if you'd rather." Darvi was the one having the difficult time, yet it was Rance who was not sure how much more he could handle. Father Confessor had never been his role with women. He had convinced himself that that type of sharing would produce too much closeness and threaten to turn a carefree physical relationship into an emotional one. Again he questioned why he had insisted on pursuing that very situation with Darvi.

She managed a brave smile. "No, I want to finish it. There's not much more to tell." Darvi wiped away the tears.

"I couldn't believe he'd actually said that. I guess I must have just stood there staring at him, my mouth hanging open. Finally he stood up and said, 'Surely you can't be expecting me to marry you.' I was in such a state of shock that my mind went blank. All I could think of was getting far away from Jerry as quickly as possible. I turned and ran blindly out the door and into the street. It was dark, raining—I ran right into the path of an oncoming car."

Her voice was quavering as she continued. "The next thing I remember was waking up in the hospital. I'd been unconscious for two days. The doctor told me I was a very lucky woman. I had sustained a bad concussion, two cracked ribs and fifteen stitches across my hip where a piece of metal cut me."

Darvi turned tear filled eyes up toward Rance's face. "There was one other little thing. I had a miscarriage—I'd lost the baby." She could not hold back the torrent of tears as they flooded from her eyes.

Her body trembled violently with convulsive sobs, the tears stung her eyes. She squeezed them shut, trying to stop the burning. Between sobs she managed to get out her final words. "I was responsible for the death of my baby—it was all my fault."

He held her firmly against him. Her last words had shocked him. His reaction was spontaneous and definitive. "No! No way were you responsible." He cupped her face in his hands, his thumbs smoothing the tears from her cheeks as he peered into her eyes. His voice was loud, his tone demanding. "Listen to me. It wasn't your fault. It was an accident—that's all."

"I...I..." She squeezed her eyes shut again as once more her body convulsed with violent tremors.

He wrapped his arms tightly around her, kept her trembling body close to his, stroked her long thick hair. Her sobs sent tears streaming down her cheeks anew. "Shh, everything's okay. You're going to be just fine." He continued to rock her in his arms.

"Hold me. Don't let go. Please, don't leave me alone."

"I'm here. I'll stay with you as long as you want me to." As he said the words he went over what Darvi had told him. So that was the basis of her anguish—guilt over a miscarriage. Two years of self-imposed hell, living with guilt and blame over something that was an accident. Darvi's sobs had quieted and she seemed to be calmer. He looked at her enfolded in his arms. She appeared so vulnerable, so in need of him.

Six

Darvi awoke with a start. Her gaze darted around the room as she collected her thoughts and got her bearings. Rance was there, on the couch with her. His arms enveloped her in a warm, protective cocoon. She looked at him, wariness and uncertainty churning through her system. Was he disgusted with her? Did he now find her beneath contempt?

He was not sure how to answer the silent pleading in her eyes. He brushed a loose tendril of hair from her cheek, then kissed her forehead. "Are you okay?"

Her wariness and uncertainty disappeared and relief flooded her as she heard what she perceived to be his reassurance and acceptance. "This is the second time in two days I've fallen asleep on my couch in your arms. I promise not to make a habit of this."

"Please, don't apologize." He studied her face. "Now, back to my question. Are you okay?"

Darvi rested her head against his chest. Her voice was quiet but firm. "You're treating me like some fragile little flower." She raised her head so she could look up at his face. "Is that the way you're going to talk to me from now on? Every time you see me you're going to feel obligated to ask me if I'm okay? I know I've been acting like an emotional basket case, but I'm not one—really."

He smiled at her. "Just humor me this one last time. Are you okay?"

"Yes, I think so." Her brow furrowed a moment. "Yes, I'm okay. This time I really mean it."

She did feel better, much better. She had been so frightened the entire time she had been telling Rance what had happened. She was afraid that he would be disgusted with her, appalled at the way she had allowed herself to be so callously manipulated. He did not seem to be either one. He did not view her with hard eyes; his touch had not turned cold. Could it be that the unprecedented chance she had taken in trusting him had paid off? It was the first time in a long while that she had put her vulnerability on the line. She did feel better, lighter in spirit, with each passing minute.

It was Rance. He had literally forced her to talk about it. He had reached deep inside her, to her most hidden vault where she had locked away her darkest secret, and yanked it out into the open. He was right; shared in the harsh light of reality it did not seem as totally overwhelming as it once had.

He took in the vulnerability in her beautiful emerald eyes, how she clung to him, the way her long copper tresses cascaded over her shoulders, how she had curled her legs under her as she sat cradled in his arms, the fullness of her firm breasts pressed against his body.

Suddenly, the full impact of his errant thoughts hit him. Darvi had just been through a gut-wrenching experience at his instigation. *And what is it you're doing, Rance, old boy? You're entertaining thoughts of lust and sex while checking out her body. Of course you want her...*

Rance's thoughts softened as he allowed his own carefully protected feelings to skirt the surface. He had wanted her from the moment he had first seen those angry flashing green eyes and that copper hair glistening in the sun, from the first time he had felt the warmth of her touch when they were introduced at the inn, from the moment he had seen her smile and heard her laugh.

He knew all too well how vulnerable she was now, how much she wanted and needed the closeness of a caring person—how easy it would be. He also knew that if he tried to take advantage of her, of the tenuous trust she had placed in him, he would be no better than Jerry Peterson. No, he would wait. They would make love because they both wanted the same thing, not because he had caught her in a weak moment.

He knew something else, too, something much deeper. He knew he cared about Darvi Stanton more than he had any other woman, and that he would go to any lengths to protect her, to keep her from being hurt again—even if his own fears and conflicts were stirred up.

The next couple of hours were spent in silence, Rance holding Darvi in the protection of his strong arms. It had been a long while since she had felt this relaxed and comfortable. She felt safe, secure—cared for.

The last light of day filtered softly through the windows as the air turned chilly. She had remained motionless for the past hour. He did not know whether she was awake or asleep. He slowly shifted his position. One arm was numb and his leg was beginning to cramp because of the uncomfortable posture he had been maintaining.

As soon as he moved, Darvi sat up. Rance immediately grabbed her hand. "I didn't mean to disturb you. It's just that—" he grinned sheepishly at her "—you've cut off my circulation. I'm losing use of some vital body parts."

She allowed a shy smile to curl her lips. "Nothing too vital, I hope." A flush colored her cheeks at her embarrassment over her own words.

"Nothing that will prevent me from doing this." He took her face in his hands and lowered his mouth to hers. His kiss was gentle—no heated passion—just the softness of tender care.

She ran her fingers across his cheek, placed the palm of her hand along the side of his face, then drew back until she could look into his eyes.

She seemed to be searching for something, asking something. "Darvi, what is it? What's the matter?"

She opened her mouth to speak, but no words came out. Indecision darted across her face. She tried again. "Rance . . . would you stay with me tonight?"

He was shocked, then surprised, and then, slowly, a warm glow of pleasure suffused him. "You want me to spend the night with you—here? *All* night?"

As his changing emotions crossed his countenance, her face became serious. "That's not what I mean."

She shyly lowered her eyelids, then recaptured his intense look. "It's just that I don't want to be alone tonight." Her eyes started to mist. "Please stay with me." She offered him the tiniest of smiles. "I've been through a lot today."

Rance searched her eyes. The panic was now gone. He saw fear, but it was different from the fear that had been there earlier. This was not the fear born of divulging a dark secret, but the fear felt when starting down an unknown path toward an unknown destination.

"Of course I'll stay with you if you want me to." He took her hand in his. "You'll be safe with me, honest."

"I know." She brushed her lips against his. Something new and exciting welled up inside her as she laced their fingers together. "I trust you."

Rance looked at the clock by Darvi's bed. It was midnight, and he was still wide-awake. He glanced at her sleeping peacefully in his arms. There had been a bit of awkwardness between them as bedtime had arrived. He had not wanted to presume he would be spending the night with her in her bed rather than on the couch. He had wondered whether he should leave his clothes on, strip to his briefs or sleep in the nude as he did at home.

He had not been able to put it off any longer, and had finally asked her, "Where do you want me to sleep?" His question had genuinely embarrassed him.

She had hesitated for an uncertain moment, then taken his hand in hers. "Come sleep with me. If you sleep out here on the couch, you might as well be home.'' As she had led him into her bedroom he had felt a tremor of panic.

Darvi stirred and Rance's attention snapped back to the present. Her face momentarily contorted into a mask of anguish, then softened as she seemed to relax. He watched her for a moment, but she did not move again. She appeared to be sound asleep. He closed his eyes and willed himself to go to sleep. Finally he drifted off into darkness.

Darvi lay quietly in bed, the predawn light just strong enough for her to make out Rance's handsome features. She studied his face as she reached out to trace his jaw with her fingers. Her gaze wandered over his broad shoulders, strong arms and muscular chest with its wisps of sandy-blond hair.

One arm of his still rested under her body and around her shoulder, where it had been all night. She felt so secure in his embrace. She watched him sleep. No one had ever shown as much concern for her as he had—not even her own family. Her mother had died when she was very young. Her father had been at a loss about raising a little girl. He had coped by keeping his distance. Consequently, he had always seemed remote and untouchable.

Darvi had talked briefly with the social worker and psychologist at the hospital following her miscarriage. It had done nothing to erase her feelings of blame and guilt, but it had given her a little insight into the dynamics of Jerry as a father figure and how that had resulted in a drive to please him so he would care about her.

Her reflections were interrupted as Rance turned over on his side, placed his other arm across her waist and nuzzled his face against the side of her breast. Darvi's nipples hardened as she felt the warmth of his breath through the fabric of her pajama top.

She knew he was asleep and was not intentionally trying to take advantage of her, but the feel of his body pressed against hers was very exciting—her skin tingled and her breathing quickened. She wanted to touch him, run her fingertips across his chest. Her desires embarrassed her. She refused to give conscious thought to the other things she wanted to do to him.

Rance gradually became cognizant of being awake. He did not move, did not open his eyes. He sorted out what had occurred the night before, where he was now, what was happening around him. He felt comfortable and warm in bed with her, even with the hands-off mode they had both silently, but mutually, agreed to. A hazy thought drifted through his sleep-clogged mind about wanting to spend the rest of his life just like this.

The feel of her fingers running lightly across his shoulder broke his moment of reverie. He remained still, reveling in the sensations her delicate touch aroused in him. He was now fully aware of just how close his face—his mouth—was to her breast. He felt the rise and fall of her breathing. He stirred, stretched out his tall frame, tightened his arms around her and drew her closer.

His body seemed to be functioning separately from his conscious control. His mouth sought out the taut nipple that protruded against the soft material of her pajama top. He gently took the nipple into his mouth, the fabric along with it. His hand moved from her waist over her pajamas and up her rib cage toward her other breast.

Darvi let out a small gasp as his mouth closed over
the delicate peak. She dug her fingers into his shoulder as she arched her back, forcing her breast more
fully against his mouth.

Rance jerked upright in a state of shock. "Darvi..."
He tugged at the wet fabric, pulling it away from
where it clung to her hardened nipple. "I didn't mean
for that to happen."

He quickly released her from his arms, running his
fingers nervously through his tousled hair as he tried
to collect his composure. He swung his long legs
around and sat on the edge of the bed as he grabbed
his jeans from the floor. After hastily pulling them on,
he turned back to her. With trembling hands he
reached down and pulled the covers up to her neck and
tucked them in along her shoulders.

He looked nervously into her eyes. "You trusted me
and I violated that trust." His brow furrowed as he
tightened his grip on the blankets. "Please forgive
me."

She reached her arm out from under the covers and
placed her hand on his cheek. Her eyes were soft, not
frightened as they had been in the past. Her voice was
quiet, yet warm and open. "There's nothing to forgive." She moved her hand along the side of his neck
and rested it gently against his chest. "You asked me
to trust—demanded I trust—and finally forced me to
trust you. You've done nothing to betray that trust."

Their eyes locked for a long moment of intense
feeling. Maybe Darvi was feeling safe, but Rance was
rapidly sinking into a panic. He tentatively encircled
her in his arms and drew her up against his body. She
returned his embrace.

Darvi slowly pulled out of Rance's arms after she glanced at the clock. "We have a meeting with Carl tomorrow morning at the inn so he can approve my designs, and I'm not quite ready for it." She turned to look at him as she spoke. Once again she placed her hand on his cheek, her fingers barely touching his skin. "Thank you for staying with me last night. It meant a lot to me not to be alone."

She studied him for a moment while turning some thoughts over in her mind. She finally formulated her words. "For two years now I've had a recurring nightmare. Whenever anything or anyone got close enough to me that I felt threatened, I'd be plagued with this nightmare until I got rid of whatever was frightening me. It's always the same. I'm being chased by a large dark shadow figure. I keep running as fast as I can, but it's always right behind me. It reaches out and is almost able to grab me. That's when I wake up, terrified, my heart pounding in my chest."

She paused for a moment before continuing. "Last night the nightmare started again." She felt Rance's arms pull her protectively against his warm body. "Only this time it didn't continue. I ran the way I always do, but the nightmare just faded out." She furrowed her brow as a slight shiver ran through her body. Her words were more of a reflection than a statement. "I don't know exactly what that means, but I hope the nightmare has finally gone away."

She leaned her face toward him and lightly brushed her lips against his. "That's why I wanted you to stay with me, why I didn't want to be alone. I was afraid the nightmare would return, in spite of everything you put me through." Her expression turned serious, her manner tentative. "I hope it wasn't too much of an inconvenience."

Rance took her hand in his, lifted it to his lips and kissed her palm. "It was no inconvenience at all."

Darvi sat at her work table, finishing the last of the watercolor renditions of her designs. Even though Carl had not officially approved them, she would go ahead and start on the full-size cartoons and the cutline tracings. She wanted to be ready to start on the actual windows as soon as possible. She had already sorted through the different pieces of colored glass she had on hand and made a list of supplies she needed to order. Her mind kept wandering back to Rance. He had reluctantly dressed and left her studio well after sunrise. As he had said when he had left, Sandy Cove was a small, close-knit town. By noon everyone would know his car had been at her studio all night.

She tried to clear the thoughts from her head, to return to her work, but she could not. Her spirits soared, her being felt so light. He was the center of all her thoughts and feelings. He had lifted her from the depths of fear and terror and raised her consciousness to a new level of strength and self-confidence. She did not have any delusions that all her fear and guilt had suddenly been swept away, but it was a start. She had not experienced such a feeling of optimism for a long time—if ever.

She leaned back in her chair, closed her eyes and allowed a sensual smile to curl her lips. Her skin tingled and her breathing quickened as she recalled Rance's warm mouth capturing her taut nipple through the fabric of her pajama top. A contented sigh escaped her lips as the sensations washed over her.

There was no question in her mind, no confusion in her thoughts. They would definitely make love—and soon.

Rance drove straight home from Darvi's studio, showered, shaved and put on clean clothes. He went immediately to his workshop. Unlike Darvi, he was ready for the meeting with Carl. He had his patterns set and had already placed an order with Frank for the additional wood he needed. As soon as it arrived Bobby could start cutting the larger pieces of the patterns. Rance had the cut list and layout ready for him. Once he was satisfied everything was in order, he started for the construction site to check in with Bill Jenkins and get a status report on the work.

As he drove he let his mind drift. An image burned into his memory—the way Darvi had looked while standing at the door of her studio when they had exchanged the first of what he hoped would be many passionate kisses. He thought back to just that morning in her bed. He smiled as he recalled the sensation of her taut nipple in his mouth.

He tried to clear the thoughts from his mind. *Rance, old boy, you have all the willpower of . . . well, I don't know of what, but you behaved like a real jerk.* As he pulled into the parking lot at the inn, his confusion over what he had gotten himself into filled his thoughts. Exactly what was his relationship with Darvi? Or, more importantly, was what he had with her really the beginning of a true relationship? An emotional melding? And if so, was it something he would be able to handle?

He felt the resentment well up as he thought about what she had told him—about her pregnancy and the final confrontation with Jerry Peterson. Her story had hit a very sore spot inside him, a spot he had carefully protected from all outside influences for the past ten years. He had allowed himself to feel again and he was scared. He shoved down the panic that was trying to establish a foothold. She was special to him. He could not turn his back on what was happening between them, no matter how much it frightened him.

Darvi's clock chimed five times as she began to clean up her studio at the end of the workday. She had finished everything she would need for the meeting with Carl at ten o'clock the next morning and had gotten a good start on the next phase of the windows. She looked at the material spread out before her and was pleased with what she saw. It was some of the best work she had ever done. She felt good about this project, confident. Once Carl approved the sketches and color schemes, the real work would begin.

She flipped on the television to catch the news as she prepared something for dinner. The weather forecast did not sound good at all. The unseasonably warm, sunny days they had been enjoying were about to come to an end. A series of storms were spread out across the Pacific Ocean and would be coming onshore one right after the other. It looked as if they were in for at least a month of cold, rainy weather.

After dinner she washed and put away the dishes, then went to her bedroom, turning out the studio lights on her way. She quickly undressed, ran a tub of warm bath water—adding some scented bath oil—and pinned her hair up on top of her head so it would not get wet. She eased her body into the tub and closed her eyes as the soothing water washed over her.

After her bath Darvi dried herself and slipped into a robe, fastening the belt around her waist. She arranged the pillows on top of her bed in a comfortable manner so she could sit up and read for a while. She had just turned the radio to a soft music station and settled in with her book, when she heard the door bell buzz.

She padded to the front door, switched on a small lamp and looked through the peephole. She was surprised, but pleased, to see Rance standing on the other side. She unhooked the night latch and opened the door, admitting him into the studio.

"Before tomorrow's meeting I thought we should do a last-minute comparison of our—" Rance stopped in midsentence as his eyes adjusted to the dim light.

The green silk robe hugged the curves of Darvi's body. The hem fell halfway down her thighs. His gaze followed the outline of her body, moved down her long sleek legs and back up to where the front of the robe gaped slightly, exposing the curve of her breast.

The delicate scent of her bath oil wafted across the open space between them, filling him with a sense of urgency. The carrying case slipped from his hand and dropped to the floor. He reached up unsteadily and took the pins from her hair, watching as the copper tresses cascaded over her shoulders.

His trembling hands cupped her face as he looked longingly into the emerald depths of her beautiful eyes. Everything that had shown in her eyes before—fear, anger, wariness, uncertainty—was gone. In their stead he saw confidence, determination and a haunting sexuality that almost knocked him back on his heels. He lowered his mouth to hers as he enfolded her in his arms. His reason for being at her studio—want-

ing to do a last-minute check before the meeting the
next morning—vanished from consciousness in a
flame of desire.

She melted in his embrace as he lowered his mouth
to hers. His lips set her on fire as his mouth captured
hers. Their tongues danced, twined, in the moist
darkness, as their breathing became labored. He held
her close, his hands moving across her back, then
dropping to her firm, round bottom. The silky fabric
of her robe hiked up higher and higher with each foray
of his hands.

She welcomed his probing tongue, the warmth of his
touch, the sensual feelings he stirred in her body. As
his hands slid over the silk of her robe, she reveled in
the sensations he created deep within her. There would
be no turning back, no stopping.

Seven

Rance felt himself slipping past the point of no return. He wanted Darvi, wanted her more than he was willing to admit, more than he had ever wanted anyone. His voice was husky as he said between kisses, "You once told me... that if you wanted me to kiss you... you'd let me know. Does that apply... to making love, too? Do I assume it's okay... do I need to ask?"

"If you don't make love to me right now—" even though the words were labored, her tone of voice teased him "—I'll never speak to you again!"

He pulled his face back from hers, a mischievous grin playing at the corners of his mouth. "I can't stand the silent treatment, so... I guess I have no choice."

He turned the bolt on the front door, and taking her hand in his, led her toward the back of the studio. Halfway across the room he stopped short, whirled around and placed his hands on her shoulders. Intense concern blanketed his features. "Darvi, I wasn't prepared for this. I don't have anything with me. Are you protected? Is it okay? Do I need to run home and get—"

She put her fingers to his lips. Her voice contained just a hint of sadness. "It's ... that won't be necessary."

Rance took her hand again. He had noted the touch of sadness, but was not sure exactly how to interpret it. "Is something wrong?" A shiver of apprehension shot through his body. "Are ... are you having second thoughts?"

She gave his hand a little squeeze and offered a shy smile. "No, I'm not having second thoughts."

He returned the squeeze, then continued on with her through the studio. As they stepped through the sliding door to her bedroom he was once again engulfed in the aura of the setting. The fragrances, the muted colors, the soft textures—they all played on his senses. He felt himself slipping into another time and place, losing himself to the soft sensuality that was Darvi Stanton.

He drew her against him, capturing her mouth with his burning need. Rance felt her hands move up under his sweater and across his chest, her touch sending tingling sensations across his body. She splayed her fingers, seeking as much of his bare skin as was possible at one time.

Darvi's senses reeled. She had never felt so excited, so alive, so desirable, so ... Words deserted her as she gave herself over to the fire Rance had lit in her. The last word to flit consciously through her mind was *love.* The word settled over her, wrapped her in a warm cocoon.

Desire surged through her as she moved her hands across his skin, pausing to tug at his sweater. She pulled the sweater off over his head as he momentarily released her from his embrace.

Rance nibbled at her mouth, tasted the sweetness of her lips, caressed her cheek and the curve of her neck. He wanted to consume her completely, totally, wholly.

He made one final stab at being sensible. That sadness he had glimpsed bothered him. His voice was husky, his breathing erratic. "Are you sure...are you really sure?"

She spoke only three words, but she murmured them in a voice so filled with desire he almost melted on the spot.

"I'm very sure."

Slowly, almost like some ancient ritual of seduction, they undressed each other. Rance stepped out of his shoes as he untied the sash around Darvi's waist. It fell to the floor and the robe parted. A sensual moan escaped his throat as Darvi's nude body met his gaze. His hands slipped inside her robe and reveled in the silky smoothness of her skin.

Darvi felt a warmth deep inside as his gentle touch expertly danced across her skin. His hands trailed over her hips, up her rib cage, across her back, down to her bottom and back up to her waist.

She unsnapped his jeans and lowered the zipper. His arousal was evident as her fingers brushed over his briefs, eliciting a gasp from him. She tugged his jeans past his hips.

Rance recaptured her mouth as his hands moved up her rib cage, then paused at her firm breasts. He cupped them, her hardened nipples pressing into his palms—and all the while, his tongue explored and tasted the textures of her mouth. He slid his hands up over her smooth shoulders, then slowly slipped off her robe, allowing it to fall on the floor at her feet. Then he laid her back across the bed. In one quick movement he kicked off his jeans and removed his briefs and socks.

Darvi stretched out her body, then reached her arms up to Rance, beckoning him to join her in the softness of the bed. He hesitated a moment, his gaze drinking in her delectable curves. The long copper tresses framed her face and fanned out over the pillow where she rested her head. Her emerald eyes sparkled with passion as she looked up at him, her slightly parted lips still wet and swollen from the feverish kisses they had shared.

Rance sank onto the bed, pulling her to him, holding her tightly against him. His voice was soft and sensual. "You're very beautiful, not only to look at and to touch, but to be with." He brushed his lips across her face—her cheeks, her forehead, the tip of her nose—to stop the words he feared he might not be able to control. "Tell me what you would like, what excites you, how I can please you."

Darvi's thoughts whirled. No one had ever asked her that before; no one had ever put her wants and needs ahead of his own—certainly not Jerry Peterson. She rubbed her bare leg against Rance's as her long fingers trailed up and down his back, sending tremors across his skin. Her voice was husky as she murmured in his ear, "How did I ever get so lucky to be here with you?"

Darvi melted into Rance's tender ministrations as he kissed the side of her neck, her throat, her shoulders. He cupped one breast and gently massaged as he sought out her other breast with his mouth. He captured its delicate peak between his lips and gently suckled, his tongue flicking across the pebbled texture.

A moan of delight escaped her lips as she arched her back, exerting more pressure against his sensual mouth. She stroked his body with her hands, his skin hot to her touch. She trailed her fingers across his hard, flat belly, marvelling at the firmness.

Rance quickly moved to suckle her other breast. His hands stroked the smooth skin of her inner thighs. A delicious shudder shot through her body and settled low in the heated center of her being. She felt his fingers twirl through the downy softness between her thighs, then slowly slip through the moist folds of her femininity.

Darvi's whimper of delight was cut off when Rance brought his mouth down hard on hers, his labored breathing matching her own. She had never before felt the level of excitement he aroused in her, experienced such all-consuming passion.

They were caught up in an inferno. Everywhere she touched him the heat was compounded. He trailed hot kisses across her body—the soft skin of the valley between her breasts, her smooth stomach. His words enveloped her. "I want to know you, touch you, taste you . . . all of you."

Darvi's entire body quivered in sweet anticipation as his lips moved down her abdomen toward the auburn curls at the apex of her thighs. When his mouth

touched the moist heat of her being she cried out as
wave after sensual wave surged through her.

With trembling fingers she reached for his hardened arousal. She heard his quick intake of breath,
followed by a moan of pure pleasure. His fingers sensually played down the length of her body. He reached
both arms around her and slowly rolled her over on
top of him. His voice was husky in her ear. "You're so
exquisite, so marvelous."

He lifted her hips and slowly brought her down on
his manhood, penetrating the velvety moist heat of her
being as he filled her with his burning desire. Darvi's
head flew back and her eyes snapped shut. The sear-
ing sensations she felt in her body made her tremble
with excitement, almost took her senses away. With
great difficulty she started to speak. "Rance...oh,
Rance—"

His mouth cut off her words as he rolled her over
onto her back, careful not to break the tangible connection between them. His hips moved in a slow even
rhythm as he wound his fingers in the long copper
tresses that covered her pillow.

Darvi moved in harmony with Rance's stroking.
Each of them felt the torrid sensations building, pil-
ing one on top of the other, until there was no holding back. They were lost in the throes of passion.

The convulsions started deep inside Darvi and
spread until she could no longer contain them. She
soared on the wings of ecstasy as their souls melded.
He had taken her beyond the limits of time and space,
to an ethereal plane somewhere on the edges of another universe.

Rance threw his head back as a growl of intense
pleasure clawed its way out of his throat. She felt his

body shudder, wracked by deep spasms, as he buried his face in her long, flowing hair and held her tightly in his arms.

A quiet euphoria settled over them as they descended from the heights. Darvi cuddled against his damp chest. She felt his breathing return to normal, as did her own. Neither seemed able to speak—nor for that matter, wanted to. They basked in the afterglow of their union, enjoying the closeness of the moment. He brushed back a loose tendril of hair that clung to her moist cheek as he pressed his lips against her forehead.

"Rance..." Darvi lifted her head from his chest.

"Shh. Whatever it is, don't confound me with mere words—I can't think straight." He stroked her hair as he looked into her upturned face. "You have me completely befuddled." He brushed her lips with his, the kiss light, but the meaning deep.

A contented sigh escaped her as she again snuggled against him. Her mind floated freely as she thrilled to his closeness. She had never felt so satisfied, so complete—so totally head over heels in love—as she did at that moment.

Rance's body may have been at rest, but his mind was wildly active. He had never felt so at one with another person in his life. He wanted to stay in her bed forever.

His thoughts bothered him. No, they more than bothered him. They petrified him, even more than he had first realized. He knew at that moment that he had been falling in love with Darvi from the first time he had laid eyes on her. The realization should have been exciting, should have warmed the cold place that had existed inside him all these years. The reality was quite the contrary, though. He heard the panic screaming in his head—telling him to get out while there was still time. He had not been looking for a relationship. He had been perfectly satisfied with his life just as it was when this woman had suddenly became entwined with his daily existence.

What to do... what to do.

He *knew* what he wanted to do, what he wanted to say to her. He gazed at Darvi nestled in his arms, then placed his cheek against her head as he let out a sigh. "What are we going to do about this? About us?"

Darvi opened her eyes, raised her head and looked at him. "Do? What do you mean by 'do about this'?" Her expression mirrored her confusion over his statement. "Is something wrong?"

He studied her for a long moment. "This wasn't my intention when I came here tonight—to end up in bed with you."

Uncertainty emanated from her green eyes. An unmistakable timbre of hurt entered her voice. "I don't understand, Rance. Are you saying you're sorry we made love? That you really didn't want to?"

He shifted his weight to his side and propped himself up on his elbow then took her face in his hands and looked searchingly into her eyes. Things were moving too fast. He did not know how Darvi felt, but he was nowhere near ready for any type of personal commitment. "I just wanted to make sure you were comfortable with what happened, that's all—that you didn't have any regrets." It was not what he had wanted to say, but it would have to do.

"No, no regrets at all."

Rance settled back into the softness of the bed, pulling her with him. She was everything he wanted, everything he needed. He began to visualize his future in entirely different terms—as a future that would include Darvi. The sensation of her fingers tickling across his bare thigh drove all thoughts from his mind—all except one. He captured her taut nipple in the warmth of his mouth as he gently stroked the smooth skin of her inner thigh.

Darvi sighed as she ran her fingers through his thick sandy hair. "Mmm. You do such marvelous things to me, make me feel so desirable and sexy." Sensual stirrings moved provocatively through her body, creating an urgency. That urgency transmitted itself silently to Rance as he lost himself in the sensations of taste and touch.

The first gray streaks of daylight challenged the night sky. Even in the dim predawn light Darvi could see through the window to the cloud cover that threatened rain. She snuggled closer to Rance as she pulled the covers up around their shoulders.

He slept peacefully, his arms still around her. She studied his handsome features, lightly ran her fingertips across the whiskers that stubbled his face, smoothed his tousled hair from his forehead. It had been quite a night. They had made love, and it had transcended anything she had ever experienced.

Even now it was like a fantasy. She feared she would wake up and find it had all been a dream. She watched as he stirred, stretched, then opened his eyes. As soon as he focused on her, he smiled and pulled her close to him. She felt so warm and safe in his arms. Life was indeed mysterious and wonderful.

Rance's voice was still thick with sleep. "Good morning." He reached his hand out to touch her cheek, to make sure she was really there. "Did you sleep well?"

"I've never slept better in my life. How about you?"

"Perfect." He rolled over on top of her, nuzzling the side of her neck before burying his face in her hair. He ran his fingers along the length of her body, thrilling to the smooth texture of her skin. He stroked her hair as he held her in his arms. "I hate to change the subject, but I have a carrying case somewhere in your studio. I wanted to do a last-minute check before today's meeting with Carl."

Darvi beamed at him as an impish grin twitched at the corners of her mouth. "Correct me if I'm wrong, but didn't we do a fairly in-depth check last night?"

"That we did, but nothing I intend to share with Carl." Rance chuckled.

"Our meeting is at ten o'clock. We'd better do something about getting ready for it." She reluctantly withdrew from his embrace. "I'll go start the coffee, then I want to grab a quick shower."

A lustful expression danced across his face. "If you don't mind, I'll use your shower while you're putting on the coffee. Then perhaps I can talk you into joining me there."

She brushed her fingers across his chest as she slipped out of bed and grabbed her robe from where it had fallen the night before. "Perhaps you can..." She gazed into his eyes, her being filled with the love she felt. "Change that 'perhaps' to a 'definitely.'" She pulled on the silk robe and headed for the kitchen.

Rance's smoldering gaze followed her. As much as he wanted to stay with her, just the two of them hidden away from the world, he knew they must turn their attention to work. If Carl approved Darvi's preliminary work, then a busy couple of months would follow. Besides, he wanted to avoid any conversation with Darvi that might center on what path their future should take. He was not yet ready to talk about that.

A cold wind whipped through Darvi as she darted across the parking lot to the construction-office trailer at the inn. She looked up at the threatening sky. It would surely be raining within the hour. When she approached the door to the trailer it swung open. Bill Jenkins was just leaving.

"Good morning, Darvi." He motioned back over his shoulder. "Carl's inside." He held the door for her, then hurried toward the inn.

"Darvi, good morning."

Carl's cheery hello and good-natured smile greeted her as she stepped inside the office.

"Good morning. It looks like it's going to pour any minute." She set her portfolio and large shoulder bag on the floor.

Carl helped her off with her jacket. "This is the kind of day that calls for a fire in the lobby fireplace. Unfortunately, the only wood we have is what the construction crew needs, so if we value our existence we'd better leave it alone." Carl looked past Darvi, out the window to the parking lot. "Ah, here comes Rance. Now we can get started."

A cold gust of wind swept through the trailer as Rance opened the door. "Whew. There's a good storm blowing up out there. I think we're really in for it."

Rance set his case next to Darvi's as he extended his hand to Carl. "Good morning, Carl. Good to see you again." After the two men shook hands, Rance immediately turned his attention to Darvi. His expression softened, his eyes taking in her every nuance. He reached out, briefly touched his fingertips to her cheek then quickly withdrew his hand. "Hi."

Rance's gesture and the look he and Darvi exchanged did not escape Carl's notice. He beamed like a proud father. "Well, I see you two are getting along much better than you were last time we got together."

Darvi lowered her eyelids as the blush spread across her cheeks. Rance shot her a quick, loving look, then returned his attention to Carl. He was all business. "Yes, I think her ideas will definitely enhance the overall aesthetics of this project. Darvi is a very talented artist. I don't think there will be any problems completing the work on time."

Carl smiled knowingly. "Of course."

For the next three hours they went through the inn room by room as Darvi showed Carl the watercolor drawings of the proposed windows and presented her color schemes and room themes. Rance gave Carl copies of the inlaid wood patterns for the doors.

When they reached the corner suites, Darvi produced drawings for three windows making up one scene that wrapped around the corner of the lower-level living room and two windows for the corner of the upper-level bedroom. It was an idea that had occurred to her the previous morning and she had worked hard on it all day long.

"Where did that come from?" Rance's voice was less than cordial as he interrupted her presentation. "You didn't run that idea past me."

Her surprise at this unexpected turn of events was immediately transformed into defensiveness and she glared at him. Her voice contained an edge of irritation. "I didn't realize I was supposed to get preapproval for my creativity. Everything that corresponds with your doors is still present in the new windows, so you won't need to make any changes in your work."

He stretched to his full height, his body language issuing his challenge and displeasure as much as his words. "I have window dimensions to consider—placement, revised blueprints. You knew that."

"The idea just occurred to me yesterday." She spit out the words in a fit of anger. "I would have been glad to apprise you of the changes last night if—" She caught herself in time, before she had blurted out the circumstances of their personal involvement in front of Carl. She saw the shifting emotions dart through his eyes and his expression soften.

Carl jumped into the conversation. "Now, now. I thought you two had signed a peace treaty." To Rance, he said, "I like the idea. There won't be any problem changing the blueprints to accommodate the new windows."

They left the inn and returned to the construction trailer. Carl put his final stamp of approval on the work presented to him. "I'm very impressed. We'll proceed exactly as you've outlined. I don't have a single change."

Carl shook hands with Darvi, then Rance. He directed his comments to Rance. "Well, I guess that does it. I'll check with you in a couple of weeks to get an update on the construction. Meanwhile, any questions or problems, feel free to call me at my Portland office."

The three of them exchanged goodbyes, then Darvi and Rance watched as Carl left the inn and hurried across the parking lot to his car. Large raindrops splattered on the ground as the sky turned even darker. Rance reached out, took Darvi's hand and gave it a little squeeze as he continued to stare out the window. "It looks like you have your work cut out for you. I don't know a whole lot about making stained-glass windows, but I do know that it'll take you a lot longer than it will for me to do the doors. Besides, I have Bobby helping me."

She jerked her hand from his grasp, surprised at his about-face in attitude. One minute he had been challenging her and the next minute he was holding her hand intimately. Her words were angry. "What was all that about? How dare you take me to task in front of Carl?"

His temper flared to match hers. "How dare you let me find out about your changes by hearing them when you present them to Carl. I have to maintain control over this project. I can't do it if the people working for me—"

Her eyes widened in shock. "Working *for you!*" She stood with her hands on her hips, as she glared at him. "I was hired by Carl, not you. And, I might add, over your loud objections!"

The clash of words and wills verged on being out of hand. They both knew there was lots of work to do and a tight schedule. Neither of them could afford this type of distraction. Their working relationship had already taken a distinct turn from strictly business to very personal, which was distraction enough.

An image popped into Rance's consciousness—that of Darvi stretched out across the bed with her arms raised toward him, beckoning him to join her there. His voice was husky, not at all in keeping with the fiery words they had exchanged just moments earlier. "All right, then...working *with* me." He grabbed her wrist and pulled her into his arms, his mouth coming down hard against hers as he infused her with all the passion flooding him.

As angry as she was with him, she could not resist his sensual aura. She melted into his embrace, willingly accepting his tongue as it probed the dark recesses of her mouth. Any lingering outrage vanished in the light of heated desire.

He flicked his tongue across her lower lip, then spoke. "I don't suppose we can do this for the rest of the day...or maybe at least through lunch?"

Eight

Their agreement to start work right after lunch had lasted only a few minutes. The increasing passion that existed between them had quickly overshadowed their good intentions. Rance kissed her bare shoulder as he trailed his fingers across her hip. He paused, his brow knitting into a frown, as he felt the scar that was the visible reminder of the night her torment had begun. He wrapped his arms around her as they shared a quiet moment following their lovemaking.

"Bill Jenkins has things under control and is actually ahead of schedule in some areas. That allows me some extra free time. I don't know very much about making stained-glass windows, but I'm a pretty quick study. Is there anything I can do to help you?"

Darvi rested her head against his chest and nestled into his embrace, his body warm beneath her. "I can't think of anything. I'm organized and have most of my materials on hand. I don't anticipate any problems with the schedule.''

He closed his eyes as he allowed the sensations of touch and smell to wash over him—the feel of her skin and long copper tresses, the textures of the lace and soft fabrics that surrounded them as they lay in her canopied bed, the combined fragrances of the various potpourri and sachets in the bedroom mingling with the scents of the bath oils in the bathroom.

Evening drifted into night as they continued to hold each other, reveling in the closeness. They talked, exchanging the details of their lives. He wanted to know everything about her, everything down to her favorite toy as a child.

''You know all about me, including my limited and unlucky history with men. What about you? Have you ever been married? Do you have any children?'' Her words were tentative, almost embarrassed. Even though he had pushed her and dug into her past, she felt as if she were intruding on his privacy.

He hesitated a moment, not sure quite what to say. It was a fair question, especially in light of the way he had badgered her. ''I was married once for seven horrible months. Joan and I had been casually dating for about three months, when she informed me that she was pregnant.'' He hesitated again, the bitter memories hard for him to verbalize. ''I thought I had taken all the necessary precautions, but I accepted what she told me as fact.'' His voice became hard. He was unable to keep his deep-seated anger from showing. ''After we were married I found out she lied to me. She made up the whole thing as a ruse to get me to marry her. I tried to make things work, but seven months later she ran off with the man she had been dating prior to me.''

Darvi saw the pain dart through his eyes. She did not know what to say. She compared his story with her own troubled past. His ex-wife had not even been pregnant, yet he had done the honorable thing and married her without hesitation. Jerry Peterson, on the other hand, had only berated and humiliated her for becoming pregnant—a rejection that still haunted her in spite of her cathartic revelation to Rance. Finally she managed a feeble ''I'm sorry'' in response to what he had told her.

''That was ten years ago.'' He stiffened. He was very uncomfortable with the direction the conversation had taken. He had let too many of his feelings show through. ''It's ancient history and doesn't matter anymore.'' Except, of course, that it still mattered a great deal—so much so that he had allowed the situation to control his life in much the same manner as Darvi's past had controlled her. He forced the sadness away and along with it his rising panic over his feeling of emotional attachment to Darvi, which was growing stronger and stronger with each passing day.

They snuggled under the down comforter as the rain continued to beat relentlessly against the roof. They shut out the world and existed solely for each other during the few remaining hours left to them before work would take precedence over their personal lives for the duration of the project.

The storm increased in intensity. The howling wind rattled the windows and the rain pounded on the roof and walls of Darvi's studio. The loud thunderclaps jarred them from a peaceful sleep. Rance switched on the lamp at the bedside. Jagged bolts of lightning streaked across the sky. The lights flickered and then dimmed.

Darvi was engulfed by a strange uneasiness. As a child thunderstorms had never been frightening. Her father had taught her to count the seconds between the lightning and the thunder to determine how far away the storm was and in which direction it was moving. This little scientific experiment had made the entire mystique less scary and more of an intellectual adventure. It was only as an adult, only for the past two years, since the night of her miscarriage, that storms like this had made her feel uneasy—and tonight was no exception.

Her body stiffened as the lights went out completely and the room was plunged into darkness. "Rance..." Her voice carried her rising sense of anxiety as she reached out for the reassurance of his touch.

"I'm here, Darvi. I'm right here. Everything's okay." He kissed her on the forehead and stroked her long hair as he rocked her in his arms. "This is very unusual, the thunder and lightning. Normally it just rains and the wind blows."

She felt a calm settle around her. Rance was with her, everything would be okay. Her body relaxed. The flashes did not seem as bright and the noise did not seem as loud.

The pendulum clock in the other room chimed three times as Rance seductively tickled his fingers up her inner thigh. The storm raged around them as they sank into the sensual swirl of their passions.

By eight o'clock the next morning the raging storm had settled into a moderate rain and the wind had subsided. Rance stood at Darvi's opened front door, sipping from a mug of hot coffee as he surveyed the scene. Trash cans littered the street; small tree branches had been broken off and scattered on lawns and across the pavement.

"You're letting in the cold air."

He quickly turned at the sound of her voice and gave her a warm, loving smile. "Hi." He held up his mug. "I took the liberty of making coffee. May I get you some?"

"Thanks, I already have." She lifted her coffee cup for his inspection, then directed her attention out the door. "How is it out there? Much damage?"

He closed the door and put his arm around her shoulder as they walked across the studio toward the kitchen. "All things considered, it's not bad. Runaway trash cans and some broken tree limbs." His brow furrowed in concentration as he glanced out the kitchen window. "However, I should get home to check out my place before I stop by the construction site to see if Bill has any significant damage to report. If it's bad, then I'm going to have to get an insurance claim filed which will not set well with Carl."

"I hope everything's okay." She looked at her watch. "According to the schedule we set up yesterday afternoon I'm already an hour behind. Looks like I'll have to work through lunch or stay overtime tonight."

He grinned at her. "The first day and already the schedule is shot to pieces." He reached for his jacket as he set down the mug. "I'd better get going. I've lots of work to do, too." He pulled her into his arms and kissed her tenderly on the lips. "I'll call you this evening."

Darvi stood at the door and watched Rance dash to his car, dodging puddles. She continued to watch until his car was down the street, turning the corner. She closed the door, then leaned against it, her eyes shut and a contented smile curling the corners of her mouth. *How did I ever get so lucky?*

The smile faded as a note of caution intruded upon her moment of happy reflection. Was she reading too much into what was happening between them? Was she hoping for more than what really existed? She shoved away the thoughts. She had lots of work to do and a tight schedule.

Rance braked the car to a screeching halt halfway up his drive. In his path were two of his trash cans and a branch from the tree next to the house. He hit the remote control to open the garage door, but nothing happened. The electricity was out.

He switched off the car ignition, took the keys and ran to the side door of the garage. He hurriedly unlocked the door and ducked in from the rain. He grabbed an old rain jacket from a hook on the door and slipped it on, pulling the hood over his head, and manually opened the garage door from the inside. Heaving a deep sigh, he ran back outside to clean the mess from his driveway.

By noon the electricity had been restored and he had swept up the debris. He called the construction site, and Bill Jenkins assured him there was no damage to speak of, no need for him to do a personal inspection. Rance was relieved things were under control. He went to his workshop to check on the progress Bobby had made the previous day. Various types of woods were stacked in the corner. Bobby had spread out the

pieces he had cut to the pattern specifications. They
were on the work bench for Rance's inspection. Rance
would do the more difficult cutting, twists and turns.
Then, like a giant jigsaw puzzle, he would assemble
the wood pieces into the desired pattern.

The falling rain hit the skylights and the sides of the
barn, creating a steady background noise. The previous night's storm had cost him a half day. There used
to be enough hours in the day to get everything done.
Now things had to be given priorities, time taken away
from this for that. He furrowed his brow and slowly
shook his head as he again wondered if he was getting
in over his head with Darvi.

Amy packaged the purchases, but held on to the bag
as Darvi tried to take it. From the moment Darvi had
entered the shop it had been obvious that Amy was
almost beside herself wanting to ask how the relationship with Rance was progressing. As Rance had said,
Sandy Cove was a small town.

Amy had followed Darvi around, making idle conversation, with Rance's name figuring prominently in
every other sentence. Darvi was not sure whether she
should be embarrassed, angry, admit everything or
pretend she did not know what Amy meant.

Amy's conversation interrupted Darvi's musings.

"And when I heard that Rance's car was in front of
your place all night, I just didn't know what to think.
Did he, uh, have some sort of car trouble?"

She looked at her friend and just shook her head in
resignation. "Amy..." She could not hold back her
amusement at being the center of gossip. She let out a
soft laugh. "No, Amy, as far as I know there wasn't
anything wrong with Rance's car." She leaned across

the counter and whispered in Amy's ear. "There's absolutely nothing wrong with Rance, either." Without waiting for Amy's reply, she took her package and left the shop, pulling the hood of her raincoat over her head as she opened the door.

Amy could not contain her excitement over the confirmation of Darvi and Rance's relationship. The words came out loud and clear, even though there was no one there to hear them. "I knew it! The moment she walked into my shop her first day in town, I knew she would be perfect for him. They were made for each other!" She reached for the phone to call Frank, unable to wait until he came home from work to share the good news.

The digital clock in Rance's workshop read seven-fifteen and he was still hard at work. He had not stopped for lunch and now it was after dinnertime. He was hungry and tired. He surveyed his work area. All the intricate pieces for two of the doors had been cut and placed in order. He made a mental note of what had been accomplished and decided things were back on schedule. He cleaned up the sawdust and wood shavings, then turned out the lights in his workshop.

After he finished dinner he almost hopped into his car and drove to Darvi's studio. He wanted to see her, hear the sound of her voice, touch her, hold her. She filled his every thought. Instead, however, he reached for the phone and dialed her number. He quickly replaced the receiver in the cradle before the phone rang. No—he was not going to put himself in the position of pursuing her any more than he already had. He had to find a balance, had to get control of the situation.

* * *

The following weeks passed quickly. Darvi and
Rance stuck to their schedules during the day, both
working at a feverish pace to finish as soon as possible. Rance had completed and hung all the custom
doors. He spent most of his time at the construction
site, overseeing the final stages of the renovations. In
fact, they were actually a week ahead of schedule, only
one week away from completion. Carl made periodic
checks on the progress and each time was more pleased
than he had been the time before.

The windows were installed in each room, but Darvi
still had to finish the lobby windows, the large size
dictating that they be done in sections. The project had
gone flawlessly in spite of the series of storms that had
swept in from the Pacific Ocean, causing power out-
ages and flooded roads.

Despite Rance's intention to slow down his growing involvement with Darvi, the two of them spent
nights and weekends, and any other time they could
spare, together. They took long walks on the beach,
wrapped in warm coats to ward off the cold wind.
They ate dinner on the floor of his living room in front
of the fireplace, warmed by the roaring flames.

On one unusually nice Sunday, they went horse-
back riding. They hiked through the woods in the
surrounding mountains. And the previous weekend he
had taken her to Portland to meet his family. They had
stayed with his sister. Rance's family adored her just
as much as she adored them.

The sight of them together had become so common
they were no longer an interesting item for the local
gossips. No one cared anymore whose car was at
whose place all night long. The thought of combining

their work and possibly their living arrangements had cropped up in Rance's mind from time to time, but he had shoved the thought away. To do that would be a form of commitment, a step he was not yet ready to take. Even though he knew he loved Darvi very much, taking that final step truly frightened him. Things were good between them as they were without the complications of commitments and plans for the future.

Darvi lay snuggled in Rance's arms beneath the flowered canopy of her bed. She kissed the warm skin of his hard chest before resting her head against his shoulder. He gently stroked her hair, then ran his fingertips across her silky skin. His voice was soft. "The inn will be finished in another ten days, by the end of next week. Carl wants to have an invitation-only open house a week from this Saturday."

She wrapped her arm around his torso. She heard his heart beating, felt his breathing. "I know. I can't believe everything that's happened in the past couple of months." She felt the flush of embarrassment on her cheeks as she realized the implications of what she had just said. "I mean, all the work that's been accomplished at the inn."

He touched his lips to her forehead and she snuggled closer to him. "I've had a call from some builders in Portland. Carl showed them photographs of the doors I did for the inn. They want me to come up and meet with them about doing some custom woodwork in a hotel they're building. I need to leave next Tuesday. I'll be gone for three or four days, but will be back in time for the open house."

She looked up at him, their eyes locking. "I'll miss you."

"I'll be staying with my sister, if you need to get in touch with me." His composure slipped as he held her tightly against his body. The thought of even three or four days away from her upset him. He was silent for a moment, afraid to speak until he had his emotions under control. "Will you be finished with the lobby windows by next Tuesday? You could come with me."

"No, unfortunately I won't be. I ran out of yellow stain. Amy had to special-order it and it won't be in until that Monday. Then I'll have about three days' work before I'm finished."

What Darvi did not tell Rance was that she had not been well lately. She felt tired, rundown and occasionally nauseous in the morning. While he was out of town she would make an appointment with a doctor and find out what was the matter. She wanted to feel at her best for the open house. She decided it was probably some flu bug that was going around. Yet in the back of her mind lurked a thought so frightening she refused to admit it to consciousness.

Rance spent the following Monday night at Darvi's before he left for Portland. For some reason—he could not put his finger on what exactly—he felt uneasy about leaving her. Something was wrong. He did not know what and she gave him no clue. Some spot deep inside him emitted warning signals, like an overpowering premonition.

Nine

Darvi sat on the edge of her bed, looking at the slip of paper Amy had given her with the name and phone number of her doctor in Summitville. A cold fear shivered up her spine as she reached for the phone.

There had been a cancellation, the receptionist said, and the doctor could take her on Thursday morning at ten o'clock. Since she was a new patient, she would have an additional half hour with the doctor to go over her medical history. Darvi gave the name of her physician in Laguna Beach so her files could be faxed.

She spent the rest of Tuesday and all of Wednesday finishing the lobby windows so the last remaining sections could be put in place on Thursday morning. The carpeting had already been installed and wallpaper hung in all the rooms. Most of the furniture had been delivered. There remained only the final decorating touches, then Saturday evening would be the open-house party before the grand opening.

Darvi's nerves played havoc with her senses as she waited in the doctor's office. The nurse had her fill out what seemed like mountains of forms, took her height, weight and her blood pressure, then showed her into a room to wait for the doctor.

"You're Darvi Stanton?"

She turned at the sound of the male voice and saw a pleasant-looking man in his midfifties. She answered, her voice sounding not as firm as she would have liked, "Yes."

He shook her hand and smiled. "I'm Dr. Hartner." He seated himself behind the desk and placed the file he carried next to the forms Darvi had filled out. He quickly glanced over the paperwork. "I see you're a friend of Amy Sutter's. How is Amy these days?"

She realized the doctor was making small talk to put her at ease, since Amy had told her she had seen Dr. Hartner just the week before. "She's fine. The art-supply shop is busy and doing well."

"That's good. I've known Amy and Frank for several years. They're nice people." He opened the file he had brought with him and looked over the entries, then closed it and looked at Darvi. "Now, what brings you here today?"

She hesitated before speaking, trying to decide precisely what to say. "I'm not exactly sure why I'm here. I've been feeling a little tired lately and sometimes my stomach is a bit queasy. I've been working pretty hard of late. I think I'm coming down with the flu."

"I see." The doctor flipped through her file. "When was the last time you saw a doctor?"

She hesitated. "It was the follow-up to my miscarriage, about two years ago."

"Well, let's get a little more information here, then we'll proceed to the examination room. Have you had any problems since the miscarriage?"

"None that I can think of."

"When was your last menstrual period?"

Darvi furrowed her brow in thought. "I guess about eight or so weeks ago, maybe longer." She considered a minute. Her voice became less confident with each ensuing word. "It was about the same time I moved to Oregon. That would be closer to three months ago."

The doctor put down his pen and gazed at her, a note of caution in his voice. "Eight weeks...maybe three months?"

She quickly interjected, "Oh, that's sort of normal for me. I was always somewhat irregular and since the miscarriage, seven weeks or so between periods has been fairly common." Her voice trailed off as her brow furrowed again. "Of course, it has been pretty long..."

Dr. Hartner looked through the file again. "I don't see any prescribed form of birth control here. Are you sexually active at this time—or have you been recently?"

She could feel the flush rise on her cheeks as she lowered her eyes in embarrassment. "Yes." Her gaze shot back to the doctor's face as she realized the implications of the doctor's words. Her voice had a sense of urgency. "But I couldn't be pregnant. After the miscarriage, the doctor said I couldn't have any more children."

Dr. Hartner again scanned the file. "I don't see any mention of that. Are you sure that's what he said?

That must have been a highly emotional time for you. Perhaps you misunderstood him. There is a notation here that you were cautioned about becoming pregnant again too soon after the miscarriage."

Panic rose inside her as her deepest fear seeped into consciousness. Her voice quavered as she spoke. "But, Dr. Hartner, I can't be pregnant."

"Oh, I'm afraid you can and very well might be. The lab will tell us for sure."

Tears welled in Darvi's eyes as she fought to maintain her control. "But you don't understand. I told Rance I couldn't have any children. I told him birth control wasn't necessary. How can I go back to him now and tell him it was all a mistake, a little misunderstanding?"

"You say 'go back to him.' Is the relationship over? Are you no longer seeing this man?"

"I didn't mean it that way. We're still seeing each other. It's just that . . ." She fought to keep control of her emotions. "How can I do this to him?"

The doctor reached over, smiled comfortingly and patted her hand. "Let's not get ourselves upset when we don't even know for sure there's any reason to be upset. Do you love this man?"

"Yes, very much."

"And does he love you?"

She hesitated a moment. "I . . . I don't know." She had never asked herself that question and Rance had never really said anything definite about his feelings. Somewhere in the back of her mind she knew she was afraid of what the answer might be.

"There shouldn't be anything the two of you can't work out if you love each other." The doctor rose from his chair. "Come on, let's find out if you have the flu or something a little more tangible."

Darvi paced up and down her bedroom, nervously waiting for Rance's call. He had phoned her every night at about this time. When he called Wednesday night he told her he would not be home until late Friday night—he had meetings all day and a dinner meeting that evening. Normally he would have stayed over Friday night and driven home Saturday morning, but he wanted to be back in time to help with the arrangements for the open house Saturday night.

She had decided not to tell him about the doctor and the probable truth of her pregnancy until the lab confirmed it. There was no reason for both of them to be upset. The lab results would be available to her Friday afternoon. When he arrived Friday night, she would know one way or the other. His words about his ex-wife's faked pregnancy played over and over in her mind, and each time she heard the anger and bitterness in his voice even louder.

Her trembling hand still rested on the phone as she sat on the edge of the bed. Her insides churned with panic; fear ricocheted through her body. Tears welled in her eyes. The lab results had confirmed her pregnancy. The probable date of conception was the first time she and Rance had made love.

She tried to remain calm, to deal with the situation logically. The first thing she needed to do was tell Rance. He would be home that night. She would tell him as soon as he arrived. Again, his angry words about being tricked into marriage filled her head and fear shook her body.

Darvi nervously paced up and down the floor as she glanced at the clock for what seemed the hundredth time. It was almost midnight. Where could he be? She had expected him home before now, even with the stormy weather and threatening rain clouds. This waiting was worse than when she had told Jerry she was pregnant. At that time she had preconceived notions of how wonderful everything would be, how happy Jerry would be at the news. This was different. She loved Rance so much. If he rejected the baby—rejected her—she did not know what she would do.

Her brow furrowed as a thought struck her. The situation now with Rance and the circumstances then with Jerry were not really that different after all. In both cases she had not thought there was any danger of pregnancy. Rance was out of town on business and did not know about her doctor's appointment, just as Jerry had not known. She looked out the window and a cold shiver went through her as she wondered what other similarities there would be.

Darvi heard the patter of the raindrops on the roof and windows of her studio. The storm came from the north. Rance had probably been driving in rain all the way from Portland. He would be exhausted when he arrived. Perhaps it would be better if she told him about the baby in the morning, after he had gotten some sleep. However, the next day was the open house. They would both be involved with the preparations and greeting and mingling with the guests. Perhaps after the party would be better. She opened the front door and tried to stare through the darkness and the rain, tried to force him to materialize from out of the night.

Rance strained to see through the windshield of his car but the driving rain made it almost impossible. Any sane, normal person would have stopped for the night, but not him. He had to get home, get back to Darvi. He had missed her so much it was almost unbearably painful. He had not realized exactly how much he loved her until he had been separated from her for the past four days. He was also worried. He still sensed something was wrong and still did not know what. He heard the stress in her voice the last time they had talked. He needed to be home with her, not out on some rain-swept road, battling the elements of nature.

Another fifty miles and he would pull Darvi into his arms. A myriad of thoughts danced through his mind, the primary theme being how he wanted the two of them to spend the rest of their lives together. A note of sadness darted through him. When she had told him she could not have any more children, the only thing it had meant to him was that he need not be concerned with birth control. But now—suddenly thoughts of a family entered his mind, thoughts he had never before seriously entertained. The thoughts confused him; he was not sure what to make of them.

Rance peered through the windshield at the winding road ahead. His body ached with exhaustion as he blinked several times to ward off the sleep that caused his eyelids to grow heavy. A soft smile curled the corners of his mouth. He had made his decision. He would tell Darvi how much he loved her right after the open house. A warm glow suffused him as he continued to drive toward his waiting happiness.

The insistent buzzing of the doorbell finally penetrated Darvi's sleep-clogged mind. She threw back the cover and rose from the couch where she had fallen asleep. She peered at the clock—it was a little after two. A gust of cold wet air rushed in as she opened the door. Rance quickly stepped inside, then closed the door behind him.

He dropped his suitcase on the floor, shed his wet raincoat and swept her into his arms in one smooth motion. His warm breath tickled across her cheek as his hands caressed her back and shoulders. His voice floated softly across her ear.

"The rain was rotten, traffic was slow and the roads were terrible. I didn't think I was ever going to get here." His mouth dropped to hers, his kiss conveying all the longing and love he felt.

It all happened so fast. One minute they stood by the front door, locked in each other's embrace, and the next minute they were in the bedroom, with Rance's clothes on the floor and his tall frame stretched out on her bed. Before she even had a chance to slide under the blankets next to him, she heard the slow, even rhythm of his breathing. He had fallen asleep.

Her eyes lovingly surveyed his tired, drawn face. He had pushed himself to the limit to be with her, rather than stay in Portland one more night. She would not wake him; he needed the rest. One more day would not matter. She decided she would tell him about the baby in the morning. She slipped into bed, nestled next to him and drifted off as his warm skin pressed against hers.

Rance sat bolt upright, the chiming clock jarring him into wakefulness. His entire being, mind and body, had shut down on him the second his head hit the pillow. He had fought to stay awake the last twenty miles of the drive. The only thing that had kept him going was the knowledge that he would soon be with Darvi—holding her, caressing her.

He grabbed his watch from the nightstand and focused on the time. He was surprised to see it was noon. He looked around. Darvi was not in bed, nor was she anywhere in the bedroom or bathroom. He climbed out of bed and cautiously peeked through the opened door, not wanting to barge naked into her studio without first making sure no one else was there.

The studio was quiet and empty. He went into the bathroom. Taped to the mirror was a note. He scanned the familiar handwriting: *Carl needed me at the inn to help with the preparations for the open house tonight. I didn't have the heart to wake you. He would like you there, too, as soon as you're up and about.*

He felt a warm glow inside as he smiled and removed the note from the mirror. He softly whispered, "I love you—more than I thought it was possible to love anyone." He paused in his thoughts as he closed his eyes and visualized her face.

Rance had made the commitment in his mind—a commitment to Darvi and to their future together. He was not happy with the arrangement of his sleeping at her place, her sleeping at his place, their sleeping apart. He wanted them to have a home together, to be a family.

He remembered the pain in her eyes as she had told him she could not have any more children. He wanted to have kids, for his and Darvi's love to produce the miracle of another life. But, if that was not to be, then that was also okay. As long as they were together, nothing else mattered. He quickly dressed, grabbed his suitcase and headed for his place. He needed to shower and change clothes.

Rance finally showed up at the inn about one-thirty, just as everyone was returning from lunch. He immediately spotted Darvi. A warm smile curled his mouth as he moved to her side, put his arm around her shoulder and kissed her cheek. "Good morning." He glanced at his watch. "Make that good afternoon. I'm sorry I conked out on you like that. I was exhausted. You should have woken me when you got up this morning."

She slipped her arm around his waist as they walked from the parking lot toward the inn itself. "You were tired—you needed the sleep. What time did you finally get up? Carl phoned me at nine o'clock and the ringing didn't make a dent in your consciousness."

"I really was out of it, wasn't I? Your noisy clock got me up. By the time it was on its twelfth chime, I was awake."

"You lolled around in bed until noon?"

He flashed her a sexy grin as he pulled her around the corner of the building. "Yeah, and it wasn't easy, either. I was alone, remember? I *loll* better when I have someone with me."

"Oh?" Her eyes sparkled. "Anyone in particular?"

"How many choices do I get?" he teased her, his heart overflowing with the love he felt for her.

She exaggerated a severe look. "You'd better not need more than one!" Darvi reached her arms around his neck as he enfolded her in his embrace, and looked lovingly into his eyes. "I missed you. I'm glad you're back." Anxiety flickered through her. Her voice was hesitant. "Rance, there's something..." She rested her head against his shoulder, unable to continue.

A tremor started deep within him and moved outward. He had been correct—something was wrong. Trepidation welled up inside him as he held her close and stroked her hair. He tried to keep his voice calm and steady, but a hint of uneasiness edged its way into his words. "Darvi, what's the matter?"

She pulled away as she gave him a brave smile. "We'd better get inside before they send a search party for us."

He did not smile and his look became very stern...almost adversarial. He refused to allow her to slip out of his embrace. "You can't put me off that easily. Something's wrong. Tell me what it is."

The smile faded from her lips and her eyes became frightened. She quickly glanced back toward the parking lot, where a couple of people were standing, looking their way. Her hands went to his chest as she pushed herself back from his arms. She made an obvious attempt to force her voice into a soft, teasing quality but was not very successful. "Rance—we're attracting an audience. We really ought to get inside with the others." Her voice softened to a whisper, almost pleading. "Please, can we go inside?"

The words were said with almost the same intonation as when she had tried to put off telling him about her past. If there was something new going on that had anywhere near the impact on her that that had, he wanted to know about it now. Almost brusquely, he said, "We're going to talk about this—whatever *this* is—before the day is through." He left no room for objection or compromise.

"Yes, we have to talk, but not right now and certainly not here." She turned and walked toward the front door of the inn, leaving Rance standing by the wall, his insides tied in knots.

Carl was a mass of nervous energy as he hurried from one room to the next. It was already five o'clock. The invitations stated cocktails and hors d'oeuvres at six-thirty, with live music and dancing. The list of invitees included city officials, everyone connected with the renovations and, more importantly, travel agents, travel magazine writers and media representatives from both newspapers and television. If people with power to entice and recommend were suitably impressed, then the success of the inn would be assured.

The caterers and musicians were on the scene, setting up their equipment and preparing for the evening. Darvi had excused herself at four o'clock to go home, take a bath and dress. Rance wanted to go with her, but she put him off, telling him she would not be that long. She assured him they would have time together following the open house. He had stood at the inn's front door and watched her walk to her car, his face mirroring his mounting anxiety.

"Rance? Are you okay?"

Amy's voice intruded on his thoughts. "What? Oh, yeah—I'm fine. Why do you ask?"

"You looked like you were on Mars or somewhere equally far away." Cautiously she continued, "Is it Darvi? Is she all right?"

He eyed her suspiciously. "Why wouldn't she be all right?"

Amy immediately realized she had said something wrong. She tried to recover. "Oh, no reason. She had mentioned being a little rundown and then when she went to see the doctor—"

The look that crossed Rance's face stopped Amy in midsentence.

"Darvi went to see a doctor while I was out of town?" he asked, stunned by the news.

Amy was now clearly nervous, flustered and apprehensive. She had said far more than she should have, had told Rance something private Darvi had not yet mentioned to him. She wanted nothing more at that moment than to terminate their conversation and return to the comfort and security of her husband's presence.

She tried to sound casual. "Oh, you know. It's probably just one of those flu things that are always going around. I'm sure it's nothing to worry about, or she would have said something." She glanced across the room. "Frank looks lost. I think he needs me." She gave Rance a tentative smile and hurried off.

Rance's heart pounded and his mind seemed unable to comprehend what Amy had said. *Darvi went to the doctor? Why didn't she tell me?* The fog began to clear from his head, and was immediately replaced by panic—full-on panic bordering on an all-out anxiety attack.

He wheeled around and walked, almost ran, to the front door of the inn and headed out to the parking lot. His single-minded purpose was to get to Darvi, find out what was wrong, determine if she was all right. *If? If? Of course she's all right...she has to be all right.* He pushed past several people, not even acknowledging them. He did not hear Carl call his name.

He sat in the parking lot with his car-engine running and the transmission in gear. Slowly he reached over and turned off the ignition. *She said we'd have time to ourselves following the open house. I'll give her through tonight to tell me about the doctor.* He slowly bent forward until his forehead rested against the steering wheel, his hands gripping it tightly, his eyes shut. He shuddered. *She has to be all right—she just has to.*

Since he was already in his car, Rance drove home and changed for the evening's festivities—even though he did not feel festive. He arrived back at the inn at six-fifteen. Darvi was already there. His eyes softened and his being filled with love at the sight of her.

She saw him standing in the doorway. Her insides were tied in knots that were growing tighter and tighter. *Does he really love me? Is it possible for him to love me as much as I love him? Will he want me after he finds out that I'm pregnant? I have to tell him. It can't wait much longer.*

Ten

Rance crossed the room to Darvi and placed his arm around her shoulder, protectively drawing her to his side. He leaned his mouth to her ear. "You look beautiful. The other women here might as well go home right now because no one will notice them after everyone gets a look at you." He fixed her with a mischievous grin. "In fact, you look absolutely delicious." He held her for a long moment, filled with the warmth and love he felt for her. "Run away with me right now. No one will even miss us."

Yet his love for her was doing battle with his anxiety over what she was hiding from him. He tried to push the anxiety aside, to focus on the happy feelings. His voice was soft and sexy as again he said, "Run away with me. We can find a private hideaway for just the two of us. The days will be warm and clear, the air filled with the fragrance of a thousand flowers. We'll take long walks in the woods and along the beach. At night we'll count the stars and make love in the soft glow of the moon. It will be just the two of us. We'll have no cares and no worries.''

Darvi rested her head against his shoulder and sighed as she laced her fingers through his. "You're very persuasive. I see and feel everything you're saying and it's wonderful.'' A hint of sadness crept into her voice. He had said it would be just the two of them. What would he say when he found that was no longer so?

He took a deep, steadying breath, then swallowed to clear his dry throat. Now was the time he would tell her of his love. He continued, tentatively and cautiously, "It is possible, you know. We can do just that. Maybe we can't stay there forever, but—''

"Hey, you two—are you going to stand here huddled in the corner, playing kissy-face forever? Guests are arriving. It's time to circulate and be charming— sell the hell out of this place!''

The abrupt intrusion had come from Bill Jenkins.

Rance looked up and saw that guests really were arriving. Some of them he recognized as locals, but others were from out of town. He looked into Darvi's eyes. "Apparently we're *on*.'' He brushed his lips quickly against hers, then added, "We'll pursue this conversation later.'' He took her hand and led her to the front door, where Carl was busy greeting the arrivals.

The evening was highly successful. Everyone had a wonderful time; the people who needed to be impressed seemed to be just that. What was supposed to have lasted until nine o'clock continued until well after one in the morning. The caterers sent out for more food and drink; the musicians agreed to stay and play as long as people wanted to dance.

Rance watched Darvi closely. She seemed to be having fun. He did not notice any tension or stress, did not notice any apprehension or anxiety. On the surface, it appeared that whatever was bothering her had vanished.

They danced to every slow song. He held her closely, reveling in the silkiness of her skin and the enticing scent of her perfume. But one thought kept repeating itself over and over—why had she gone to the doctor and why had she not told him?

It was well after midnight when he spotted Darvi in a far corner huddled with a stranger, a man he had never seen before. They seemed totally absorbed in their conversation. Rance made his way across the room to where they stood.

Darvi smiled at him as he approached. "Rance, this is Barney Wilton." She turned her attention to Barney as the two men shook hands. "Rance was the contractor on this job. He also made all the custom-designed wooden doors for the rooms."

She directed her comments to Rance. "Barney's a contractor, too. He came with his wife this evening. She's a travel agent. Barney and I were discussing a house he's remodeling in Summitville. The owners have expressed an interest in some stained-glass window insets for the double doors at the entrance. I'm going to drive over on Monday and take a look at what they have in mind and see if I can come up with something they'll like."

Darvi turned her attention to Barney as she held up his business card. "I'll stop by your office about ten o'clock Monday morning, if that's okay."

Barney extended his hand to Darvi. "I look forward to it." He turned to Rance and shook his hand. "Rance, it was a pleasure." He glanced toward the inn's front door. "Now, I'd better catch up with my wife before she runs off and abandons me."

They watched as Barney walked across the lobby, then Darvi said to Rance excitedly, "He really liked my work. He says he has several projects in the planning stage and might be able to use my talents often." She smiled at the prospect. "Isn't that thrilling? I was a little worried when I moved up here—wasn't sure exactly how much work I'd be able to generate."

He put his arm around her shoulder and gave a squeeze as he smiled at her. "That's great." A sudden thought hit him. "Hey—why don't I go with you on Monday? I don't have anything to do that can't wait until Tuesday. We could stay and have lunch in Summitville before driving home."

A cloud of apprehension settled over her. She spoke hesitantly. "Actually, I have some personal errands to run—it would just be boring for you." She offered him a reassuring smile. "I promise to be back by early afternoon." What she had not offered him was the complete truth. She had a personal errand all right—another appointment with Dr. Hartner.

Rance furrowed his brow. *She blatantly put me off with a flimsy excuse. She doesn't want me to go to Summitville with her. Why?* He tightened his hold on her, a shiver of fear darting through him. "Sure, that will be okay. I do have some preliminary designs to do for the Portland project."

Darvi's face lit up. "Oh! Did you get the job?"

"I don't have a signed contract yet, but we shook hands on it."

She threw her arms around his neck as she beamed her happiness. "I'm so thrilled about your news." She clung to him for a moment longer. *I hope you'll be thrilled about mine.*

He held her to him and felt the tension in her body. He spoke softly in her ear. "Let's go home. I have something I want to say to you and this isn't the place."

The churning in her stomach returned; the knots grew tighter and tighter. *He knows—somehow he knows!* Total panic set in. *I'm not ready to discuss this yet! I've got to put him off until after the doctor's appointment Monday.* She put her hand against his cheek. "I'm very tired—it's been an incredibly busy day. Could whatever it is keep for a while?"

Her eyes showed how frightened she was as he peered into their emerald depths. An intense battle raged within him. He was torn between demanding to know what was wrong and giving her the room she was desperately seeking. He rested his cheek against the top of her head and let out a sigh. "I don't know what this is about, but you seem to want some space, some time."

He pulled back and looked into her very soul. "I'll give you the space, but I can't give you very much more time." He pulled her to him again, as his own pain and anguish showed in his voice. "I'll give you until Monday evening. If you haven't told me what this is about by then I'm going to pester you nonstop until you confess everything. I won't give you a moment's rest until I know for sure that everything's all right."

Her voice was soft and quiet. "Fair enough."

"Do you want to be alone tonight?" He was not sure where the question had come from. The reality was that he wanted to know exactly what was going on with her and he wanted to know now.

"No." She had never been so frightened in her life. She could not put off the inevitable much longer.

They lay under the flowered canopy of her bed. His arms were wrapped around her, her body rested next to his, their bare skin touched. They had not made love, even though it had been almost a week since they had shared the intimate joys of their togetherness. Rance held her the way he had the night he had forced her torment out into the open.

His thoughts were a mass of confusion. He wanted so much to tell her he loved her more than life, but he was afraid even to broach the subject until they had dealt with whatever it was that had her so worried. Neither spoke; they simply lay quietly until sleep claimed them.

Rance and Darvi walked across the lobby of the inn. Storm clouds threatened on the horizon as they made their way to the cozy setting by the fireplace where Amy, Frank and Carl—who had stayed over rather than make the late night trek back to Portland— waited for them. It was smiles all around as they greeted everyone.

Carl held up his coffee cup. "I'd like to propose a toast. To all of you and everyone else who worked so hard to make last night's effort a great success. Words alone can't express how much I appreciate your efforts."

He put his cup down on the end table next to his chair. "I've been getting feedback all morning and every bit of it is positive. There will be a two-page spread in the travel section of next Sunday's Portland newspaper—" they all beamed their pleasure at the news "—and two weeks from today the Sunday magazine supplement of the Seattle paper will carry an article with color photos. The San Francisco paper will be doing the same thing.

"And you two—" Carl looked at Rance and Darvi "—I can't begin to tell you how many words of praise I heard about your work. Everyone loved it. The stained-glass windows are beautiful." He addressed his next comments to Rance. "This is the smoothest construction job I've ever been involved with. You had a top-notch crew and everything was very professional and first-class. I'm glad you talked me into the custom-designed doors. They added just that special touch to the hallways."

"Thanks, Carl. That's nice of you to say." Rance smiled at him, then looked at Darvi and gave her hand a squeeze.

Everyone was in high spirits as they talked about the previous night's open house. Darvi excused herself a couple of times to go to the rest room. The second time, Amy quietly excused herself and followed.

In the rest room, Amy immediately turned to Darvi. "Does he know yet? Have you told Rance?"

Darvi feigned ignorance at her question. "Does Rance know what? What are you talking about, Amy?"

Amy looked at Darvi for a long moment. "I'm talking about your being pregnant."

Darvi's eyes opened wide in shock. "But how—"

Amy put her arm reassuringly around Darvi's shoulder. "It's so obvious. You know, Rance is worried sick about you. Whenever he thinks no one is watching, his entire face shows his concern. Don't you think it's time you told him?"

"Oh, Amy, I don't know what to do." She sank into a chair as tears welled in her eyes. "It's more than just my being pregnant. All I keep thinking about is the situation with his ex-wife."

The confusion covered Amy's face. "His ex-wife? Rance has been divorced for about ten years. What would his ex-wife have to do with this?"

"Didn't you know? She tricked him into marriage by telling him she was pregnant. You can't imagine the anger and bitterness in his voice, even after all these years, when he told me about it. What if he thinks I'm doing the same thing?"

"I can't believe Rance would think that of you. You have to tell him before any more time goes by."

"Of course I have to tell him—I just don't know how."

After about fifteen minutes the two women returned to the lobby. As they sat down, Frank glanced at his watch, then at Rance. "Have you ever noticed that one woman in a bathroom takes twice as much time as any man, but two women in a bathroom..."

Amy glared at him, then broke out in a laugh. "This, coming from a man who takes half an hour just to decide what temperature he wants the shower."

Everyone's spirits seemed light, but Rance's demeanor held a note of caution. He watched Darvi carefully, looking for any signs that would tell him what was going on, what was wrong. He was positive she and Amy had been talking about it. After all, Amy

had known she had been to the doctor. What was it
that she could confide in Amy and not tell him?

It was midafternoon before they left the inn. Carl
was the one who finally broke up their group. The
storm clouds were moving in; the wind had become
stronger and colder. It was definitely going to rain a
good one before the day was out and he needed to get
on the road back to Portland before he got caught by
the elements.

Darvi and Rance hurried to the car, the cold wind
whipping around them. He held her hand as they
drove to her place in silence.

Rance stood inside Darvi's front door, preparing to
leave. "Now remember, you have only until tomorrow evening to tell me what's going on here." He was
torn between leaving her alone for the night, as she
had requested, and demanding then and there that she
tell him what was bothering her.

He looked at the blackening sky and threatening
storm clouds. "It looks like we're in for a good
downpour. Are you sure you want to be alone? I could
stay. I promise I'll be as quiet as a mouse."

She placed her hand lovingly against his cheek as
she stood on her toes so she could reach his mouth.
She brushed his lips with a kiss. "It isn't whether or
not you're making noise—your mere presence is totally distracting to me." She looked into his eyes, silently pleading for just a little more understanding,
just a little more blind faith. Her voice was a mere
whisper. "I can't think when you're around me."

He scowled. "I don't like it, Darvi. I don't like
knowing something is wrong and your not telling me
what it is." His expression was stern and his words

clipped, almost as if he were barking out an order. "Remember, tomorrow evening and not a minute longer."

His manner softened as he wrapped her in his arms. His mouth captured hers, the kiss lasting only a moment. "I'm just a phone call away if you need me." He forced a smile, not at all as confident as the image he projected.

They held each other's look for a few seconds, then he opened the door and left. A strong gust of cold damp air made her shiver before she could close the door behind him. Darvi walked slowly into her bedroom, her mind racing in a thousand directions at once as she pondered her dilemma: *How do I tell him that he's going to be a father? That I'm carrying his child? What will he think? How will he react?*

Rance lay in bed, staring up at the ceiling. He had been berating himself from the moment he had arrived home. He never should have left her, never should have allowed her to talk him into leaving her alone. He continued to stare at the ceiling as his eyelids grew heavy. Finally he drifted into an uneasy sleep.

The storm hit about eleven o'clock that night. The rain pounded against the windows and on the roof. Darvi lay in bed, listening to the howling sound the wind made as it whipped around the studio and through the trees. She huddled under the covers, feeling very lonely in the large bed. She had become so accustomed to Rance's body next to hers as she slept, his warmth radiating to her, his strength being hers.

She had made her decision about how to tell him. There was no reason to wait until after the doctor's appointment. She would just say it straight out and hope he accepted it without being upset or angry. Even if the lab had made an error and she was not really pregnant he still had to be told she was not protected against future pregnancy—they must take precautions.

Darvi climbed out of bed. She never should have let Rance go home. She would drive to his house. She wanted the comfort of his arms. She wanted to tell him now about the pregnancy...she wanted to tell him that she loved him. She dressed quickly, then darted through the rain to her car.

The insistent buzzing of the doorbell finally shook Rance out of his sleep. He pulled on his jeans, went to the door and angrily yanked it open. The cold air hit his bare chest and bare feet.

"Darvi!" He reached out and pulled her inside, quickly closing the door behind her.

She tried to sound calm and in control. "We have to talk. It can't wait any longer."

Something about her expression and the stress he heard in her voice immediately put him on alert. His tone held a hint of caution as he measured his words. "Of course, but why didn't you call? I would have driven to your place. You shouldn't be out in this weather. The roads are far too dangerous."

"I...I've put this off too long as it is. It can't wait any longer."

Rance felt a tightening across his chest as apprehension seeped into his consciousness. Rather than pulling her securely into his embrace, he stepped back and folded his arms across his chest. He did not seem to have any control over the cool tone that surrounded his words. "So, what seems to be the problem?"

Darvi was taken aback by this surprising change in attitude. Rance had become distant. He had backed away from her and was not providing any physical comfort. Did he suspect the truth? Were her own fears dictating her thoughts, or was he already blaming her, thinking she was attempting to manipulate him just as his ex-wife had?

She swallowed hard, trying to ease the lump in her throat. She searched his face for some clue to his feelings, his mood. She saw what looked like thousands of thoughts and emotions darting through his eyes—all of them enveloped in caution and uncertainty. She began to tremble as her worst fear filled her being.

"Well, I went to the doctor last week and...uh...he did some tests and..." Her gaze darted nervously around the room, landing briefly on some object, then moving quickly to another. Her hands twisted the bottom of her sweatshirt, her mouth went dry, her stomach churned.

"And what?"

There was a hard edge to his voice. His look was so intense it frightened her. She was unable to continue.

His voice grew louder... and angry. "And what, Darvi? What's going on here? You went to the doctor and he did some tests—then what? Come on, out with it!"

She twisted her face in anguish and clamped her eyes shut. She forced the words out, her voice barely audible. "I'm pregnant. I'm almost eight weeks along."

There was a long moment of silence before he responded to what she had said. His voice was remote, disconnected, unbelieving. "What do you mean you're pregnant? How could this happen?" His mind was lost in a whirlwind, failing to fully comprehend what she had said.

Darvi did not know what his reaction to the news would be, but this certainly was not what she had expected. She was not sure what to do. She knew only that she was solely responsible for her condition. Rance had asked her and she had told him it was safe, that he had nothing to worry about. That put the responsibility squarely on her shoulders.

All the defensiveness that she used to hide behind suddenly sprang to the forefront again. "I understand it's a possible side effect having something to do with engaging in sexual intercourse." Her voice was caustic, but she could not hide the tinge of pain.

"Don't be flippant with me, Darvi. You know exactly what I mean." All the bitterness and anger associated with the circumstances of his short-lived marriage flooded into his mind. "What the hell's going on here? What are you trying to pull?" He may have been talking to Darvi, but in his mind he was seeing Joan coyly batting her eyelashes and telling him she had not really been pregnant.

Darvi's heart pounded; her stomach churned and knotted. She felt physically ill. Her mouth and throat were dry. Her mind tried to go blank, to deny what she had just heard and seen—to shut out the incredible pain that stabbed at her being. Her eyes widened with fear as her fingertips went to her lips. The words tumbled out. "Dear God...please, not again. Oh, no—it's just like Jerry Peterson." Tears filled her eyes and her purse fell from her hand as she whirled around, yanked open the door and dashed out into the darkness. He was rejecting her, just as Jerry Peterson had done two years ago.

The rain pelted her face as she ran blindly toward her car. Her tears stung her eyes. Her sobs choked in her throat. Numbness invaded her consciousness as she tried to block the unbearable pain.

A terrifying, sinking feeling lodged in the pit of Rance's stomach as he stood in the doorway. He was frozen to the spot, unable to force himself into any type of action. He had never in his life experienced the type of emotional turmoil that gripped him at that very moment as he watched her car's taillights fade from sight.

Eleven

Rance sank into the couch as he tried desperately to sort out what had just happened. He sat motionless for a long time, his mind clouded with bitter and angry memories from the past that tried to force themselves onto the reality of the present. How could Darvi have done this to him? She had actually tried to pull the same scam as his ex-wife. The only difference being that, unlike Joan, he loved Darvi more than he was able to fully comprehend or explain. He felt empty inside, as if his life had been drained off and there was nothing left for him.

It must have been a full fifteen minutes before he was able to rise from the couch and get his mind working. Joan was history—that entire nightmare had been ten years ago. He had held on to it for too long. It was time to let go—to replace it with something new.

Darvi was now. She was more important to him than anyone—he loved her.

The crystal-clear reality of what had happened and what he had done exploded in his head. Panic raced through him. He had actually stood in the doorway and allowed the woman he loved to drive off into a storm without doing a thing to stop her. Her final words rang loud and clear in his ears. She had compared him to Jerry Peterson, a man who had cruelly rejected her in her time of need—a despicable act no decent man would do. He closed his eyes and clenched his fists, the thoughts ripping his insides to shreds—a despicable action that he himself had just inflicted on the woman he loved more than he was capable of expressing.

He forced his body to move as he broke out of his stupor. He raced for the phone and dialed her number. He let the phone ring twenty times before he hung up. He glanced at the clock. More than enough time had passed for her to have gotten home. He dialed again, hoping he had misdialed the first time. Another twenty rings, and still no answer. He tried to alleviate his growing anxiety by telling himself she was understandably angry with him and was probably refusing to answer the phone. He silently prayed that was the reason.

The trepidation built inside him as he quickly dressed. He drove straight to Darvi's studio. Her car was not there; the studio was dark. He pounded on the door and rang the bell. No one answered. He took the key she had given him and entered the studio. Everything was quiet. He quickly moved through each room, turning on lights, calling her name. She was not there.

He stood at the front door, trying to peer through the darkness and rain. He ran over all the possibilities, any place she might have gone. A thought clicked in his mind. He grabbed the phone and dialed Amy.

Frank's sleepy voice growled into the phone. "This'd better be important."

"Sorry, Frank. It's Rance. I need to speak to Amy and yes, it's important."

Even in his half-asleep condition, Frank recognized the urgency in Rance's voice. "Sure thing, I'll get her."

A moment later, Amy came on the line. "What is it, Rance? Is something wrong?"

"Is Darvi at your house?"

"Here? No, she's not here. I haven't seen her since we were all together earlier today." Amy's voice took on a note of concern with a hint of urgency. "What's wrong?"

"Damn!" He paused as he tried to think. "Where would she go, Amy? Where could she be?"

"I don't understand. Is she missing? What's happened?"

"She came to my house late this evening. When she left she was extremely upset. She drove off in the rain. I can't find her anywhere and I'm very worried. I'm at her studio right now. She didn't go home. I thought maybe she had gone to your house."

"Oh, no. Rance, what did you say to her? I know she was very worried—she didn't know how you were going to take the news."

Her words caught him totally by surprise. His temper exploded before he could stop it. "What is this, Amy? Does everyone in town know about it?"

There was a long silence on the other end of the line.

"Amy? Amy, are you still there?"

Amy's tone was curt, showing her extreme displeasure with his attitude. "Yes, I'm still here and no, she didn't tell everyone in town. She didn't even tell me. I guessed it. I don't understand you, Rance. Is that the tone of voice you used with her? The attitude? No wonder she was so frightened at the prospect of telling you."

Amy's accusations hit him with a hard slap. Darvi had been afraid to tell him? He had realized that she had been upset about something, but her being afraid to talk to him had never occurred to Rance. He took a calming breath before continuing. "I'm sorry, Amy. I didn't mean to snap at you like that. It's just that this entire thing came out of left field. I...well, I didn't take the news in a very compassionate and understanding manner." His voice took on a new sense of urgency. "I've got to find her. She can't be out wandering around in this storm—alone, frightened and thinking I've rejected her. Do you have any idea where she might have gone?"

"No...none."

"Do me a favor. If she shows up at your place, don't let her leave. I'll check with you later."

"Good luck, Rance. Call if there's anything I can do."

Rance leaned forward, resting his elbows on his knees, his head in his hands. A dark fear seeped into consciousness. He raised his head and opened his eyes as it spread through him.

"Sandy Cove Sheriff's Station."

Rance's impatience bristled across the phone lines. "Sergeant Maxwell, and hurry." It seemed like hours before the familiar voice came on the line.

"Maxwell."

"Tom, it's Rance. I need your help, right away."

"Sure, buddy. What's the problem?"

"It's Darvi. I can't find her. She left my place in a very distraught condition. She's out in this storm somewhere. Could you check, see if any of your deputies have spotted her car—maybe she had car trouble somewhere, or something…" His voice trailed off as other possibilities darted through his mind. Then he remembered seeing her purse drop to the floor. "She doesn't have her purse with her—no money, no identification."

Tom's voice took on the air of authority that went with his job. "Sure thing. We'll also check the Summitville hospital—" He stopped in the middle of his sentence as he heard the quick intake of breath on the other end of the line. His voice softened, became comforting. "That's just routine procedure, Rance. I'm sure she's okay. She's probably someplace safe, warm and dry—just waiting for the storm to lift so she can go home. Don't worry."

"Yeah, I'm sure you're right." He lacked any enthusiasm for his words. "Thanks, Tom. Call as soon as you hear anything. If I'm not home, leave a message on my machine or call Amy Sutter and leave a message with her."

Rance slammed the door of his truck as he jammed the key into the ignition. He was not sure where he was going, but he knew he could not just sit still and do nothing. He drove the truck slowly down the street, carefully checking each vehicle he came across, making sure it was not Darvi's car. He covered every possible route between his place and hers, checked every parking lot of every store, scoured the road to the main highway and back.

Just south of town he hit his brakes and skidded to a halt on the rain-slickened pavement, gripping the steering wheel so tightly his knuckles turned white. He spotted Darvi's car off the side of the road, halfway in a ditch. His heart pounded. It felt as if it would burst out of his chest at any moment. He leaped from the truck, not even turning off the engine, and raced toward the disabled car. The cold, driving rain stung his face as the wind howled in his ears.

He yelled into the wind. "Darvi! Darvi, are you all right? Answer me! Darvi!" The howling wind carried away his desperate cries. As he reached the car he lost his footing in the mud and slid down the side of the ditch, tumbling until he landed at the bottom in a pile of muddy debris and a tangled thicket of brush.

He clawed his way up out of the ditch, grasping at whatever he could find to help pull himself along. His clothes caught on something. He heard fabric rip and felt a sharp sting in his left leg. The muddy gravel scraped the side of his face as he again lost his footing and slid back into the ditch.

He tried once more, climbing to the top of the ditch, then grasping the side-view mirror on her car to steady his position. It was the passenger door. He tried to open it, but it would not give way—it was locked. He carefully skirted the car, banging on the windows and hood, calling her name.

Rance yanked open the driver's side door. The car was empty; the keys were not in the ignition. He raced back to his truck, retrieved a flashlight, clicked it on and began searching the area around the vehicle. He looked in all directions, but found nothing.

He was frantic. Was she all right? If she was okay, then where had she gone, and if she had been injured—again, where could she be? His clothes were soaked through to his skin. He was muddy from head to toe and cold. The side of his face and his hands were covered with ugly scrapes and scratches. His ripped jeans exposed a nasty gash across his thigh from the fall into the brush pile. Only his adrenaline kept him from folding...and his desperate need to find Darvi, to know she was safe.

Bright headlights appeared from around the curve of the road and headed toward Rance. A squad car pulled alongside him and Tom Maxwell rolled down his window. "Did you find her?"

Rance had to yell to make his words heard above the howl of the wind. "This is her car, but she's not here. I've searched the area and I can't find her. Have you heard anything?"

"We've checked the hospital and local doctors and no one answering Darvi's description has shown up. Are you sure this is her car?"

"Positive. In fact, that's my sweater in the back seat."

"Hey, she probably caught a ride with someone and is home right now. I'll have my men keep their eyes open, but I'm sure she's okay." Tom glanced down at Rance's leg. "Speaking of doctors and hospitals, you'd better get that leg of yours taken care of. It looks pretty bad."

Rance was puzzled. "What leg?" He glanced down and saw the nasty gash and blood. He had not even realized he was hurt. "No. I've got to find Darvi first. I'll be okay."

"I'm going back to the station. Let me know if you locate her and I'll give you a call if I hear anything." Tom rolled up the car window and headed down the road.

Rance returned to his truck and headed back up the road toward town. As he passed the inn a glimmer caught the corner of his eye. Visibility was terrible—he was not even sure he had really seen something. He made a U-turn and pulled into the inn's parking lot. Yes, he could see it. Through the front windows of the lobby he could discern a faint glow coming from the back storage room.

He felt the first stirrings of hope. Darvi still had a key to the inn's front door. The inn was less than half a mile from where he had found her car. She could have walked here. If she had been able to walk that distance through the storm, then she was all right.

Rance shoved through the unlocked front door, the wind whipping in behind him. A gust caught the door and slammed it shut. He stood still, listening. He heard only the howling wind and the pounding rain. He moved quickly toward the light, holding his breath, hoping against hope.

He reached out and pushed open the partially closed store-room door. He was afraid to breathe as the door swung wide. All his hopes were dashed; his heart sank. The room was empty.

The store-room light was just bright enough to break the darkness and be seen from the road. The furniture blankets were piled against the far wall. They had been left behind when the furniture had been delivered a couple of days before the open house.

Rance looked again. He blinked, clearing his eyes. He wanted to make sure he saw correctly. His heart beat faster as the full impact of what he was looking at pierced his consciousness. The blankets were not folded—they were bunched in a wet, muddy pile. His eyes opened wide. He quickly stepped into the room. As he cleared the door a quick intake of breath met his ears. He whirled around and there behind the door, holding a fireplace poker at the ready, stood Darvi. He saw the fear leave her eyes and the frightened look on her face soften as she focused on him.

He grabbed her, pulled her into his arms and held her close against him. "Thank God..." He rained what seemed like thousands of kisses over her face and neck. "I've been looking everywhere for you. I was scared to death...finally found your car..." He held her to him, almost crushing the breath from her lungs.

Even though she felt an enormous sense of relief as soon as she saw that the intruder was Rance, the terrible hurt that filled her being did not lessen. She struggled in his arms, attempting to free herself from his tight embrace. She shoved her clenched fists against his hard chest as she unleashed her anger. "Let go of me! Just leave me alone—I don't need you."

He pinned her arms to her side and held her tightly. He barked out his words as if giving an order. "Stop it, Darvi! We have to talk."

She continued to struggle against his iron grip, refusing to look at him. Tears streamed down her cheeks. She forced out her words between sobs. "There's nothing to talk about. You've already made your feelings perfectly clear. Now, get out and leave me alone!"

He turned her loose and took a step back. Her angry words stung like barbs. He made a frantic search of his mind in a desperate attempt to remember ex-

actly what he had said to her. He knew he had blurted
out something—angry words that had come from his
own deep-seated pain. The anguish on her face and the
pain in her eyes cut through him like a sharp knife.

He ran his fingers through his muddy, wet hair and
tried to gather his thoughts, as the chill of his soaked
clothes settled over him. A stab of pain buckled his
leg. He grimaced and fell back against the wall, a
groan escaping his lips as he slumped to the floor.

Darvi immediately knelt at his side. Her deep concern colored her voice, her love for him temporarily
driving away her hurt and anger. "Rance, what's
wrong?"

"My leg. I didn't feel it until now." Another grim-
ace shot across his face as he grabbed his left thigh. "I
guess I was so intent on finding you that I blocked out
the pain." He tried to smile, make light of the injury.
"It seems to be making up for lost time now, though."

For the first time, Darvi saw the bleeding gash.
"Rance!" She pulled at his arm and took immediate
control of the situation. "Come on, we've got to get
you to the doctor. That wound needs to be cleaned.
You need stitches and a tetanus shot."

"I'll be okay. Just let me rest for a moment."

"Forget it, buster. We're going to the doctor right
now. Where's your car, in the parking lot? And I hope
it's your truck instead of your car. It will have better
traction on these wet roads."

"Yeah, it's my truck and it's in the drive right by the
front door." The full impact of what she was saying
finally hit him. He looked up at her in amazement.
"You don't think I'm going to let anyone other than
me drive my truck, do you? You've already run your

car into a ditch. I won't have my truck suffer the same fate.''

Her anger flashed again. "First of all, I didn't run my car into a ditch. Another car came around the curve too wide and ran me off the road." She calmed down as she again looked at the nasty wound on his thigh. "You and that precious truck of yours. You don't think for a minute that you're going to be able to handle the gas pedal, brake pedal and clutch with that leg, do you?" She reached out her hand and snapped her fingers in front of his face, then opened her palm. "Give me the keys."

"I can handle it just fine." Rance rose to his feet, then grimaced again as he tried to put his full weight on the injured leg. He held out his arm as he leaned back against the wall, a hint of embarrassment crossing his face. "I think you're going to have to give me a hand."

She took in the man leaning against the wall. His clothes were a wet, muddy mess, his face and hands were scratched and scraped, his hair was plastered to his head and he had a bleeding gash in his thigh. The love she felt for him far outweighed her pain and anger. The harsh edge disappeared from her voice. "You look like you need someone to take care of you— you're a mess."

He wiped a smudge of mud from her cheek. "Take a look in the mirror—you're no glamour queen yourself at the moment." His voice softened as the love he felt for her welled up inside him. "I don't need *someone* to take care of me—I need you to take care of me."

They held each other's looks for a long moment. His words came out in a rush as he was overcome by emotion. "Don't ever run off from me like that again. When I couldn't find you, I was frantic. I have half the county out searching for you."

A sudden blast of cold wind whipped through the lobby and into the store room. The sound of the howling wind became much louder, then quieted again as the lobby door opened and closed. Someone had entered the inn. Rance and Darvi both tensed as he immediately turned toward the door, moved her protectively behind him and motioned for her to hand him the poker.

"Hello—sheriff's department. Is anyone in here?"

They each expelled the breath they had been holding and emitted a sigh of relief. Rance pushed open the store-room door. "In here."

The deputy walked through the lobby. "Well, I see you found her. Is everyone all right?"

"Yeah, we're fine. Nothing a good hot shower and some clean clothes won't fix."

Darvi quickly interrupted. "One of us is fine. The other one needs to get to a doctor."

The deputy glanced down at Rance's leg, then at Darvi. "Can you take him, or do you want me to drive him to Doc Bradford's place?"

"Help me get him out to his truck. I can take it from there."

"Hey!" Rance was clearly irritated. "The two of you are talking about me as if I weren't even here. I can get me to my truck and I can get me to the doctor—*if* I decide that's what I need to do—all by myself."

The deputy continued to address his comments directly to Darvi, ignoring Rance. "Sergeant Maxwell told me he'd probably say something like that."

"Yes, he's very pigheaded. Give me a hand."

The deputy stood on one side, with Darvi on the other, as they helped him across the lobby, with Rance all the while insisting he could walk on his own.

It was almost daybreak by the time they left the doctor's office. The wound was not as bad as it had originally looked, once the doctor cleaned out the mud and splinters. It had required only a few stitches. The doctor warned Rance it would be pretty sore for a couple of days and he should change the dressing regularly. Then the doctor gave him the tetanus shot he kept maintaining he did not really need.

The main fury of the storm had subsided, but it was still raining, and it looked as though it would continue throughout the entire day. Darvi drove them to his house. Conversation between them was strained, Rance trying to banter and Darvi keeping silent. When they got to his place she retrieved her purse, still on his living-room floor where she had dropped it in her hasty departure the night before. He checked the messages on his answering machine. There were four from Amy, two from Tom Maxwell, one from Frank saying Amy was too upset to make her fifth call and one from the all-night service station on the main highway, saying the sheriff's department had told them to get Darvi's car out of the mud and Rance would pay the tow.

He glanced at his answering machine. "I seem to have several phone calls to take care of. Why don't you take my truck and go on home so you can clean up? I'll grab a quick shower and join you shortly." He saw her stiffen and a wary look come into her eyes.

''Please, Darvi. We have to talk. We have to straighten this out.''

She stepped back from him before he could wrap his arms around her. She steeled herself against his all-too-tempting nearness. ''Your injury has been tended to and you've been delivered home. As far as you and I are concerned . . . well, I believe you've already said everything there is to say.'' She placed the keys to his truck on the table, then turned toward the door. ''I can get home by myself.''

He reached for her arm, but she moved out of his grasp and walked out the door—once again disappearing into the rain.

Darvi stepped out of the rose-scented bathwater as she wrapped a large bath towel around her body. She grabbed another towel, rubbed the excess water from the tangled mass of copper that was now at least clean. She picked up her hair dryer as she combed out the tangles.

She mechanically worked at her hair, her thoughts centering on everything that had happened during the previous twelve hours. She needed to keep her head clear, to crystallize her thoughts. Her first priority should probably be to move to another town. Sandy Cove was a small community. She could not continue to live and work here without running into Rance on a regular basis. She could not raise her child in such a strained atmosphere, where she and her baby would be subjected to his ongoing presence and rejection. She continued to dry her hair as she fought desperately to keep her deep sorrow from taking over.

She glanced at the clock. It was already after eight-thirty in the morning. She had not gotten any sleep the previous night. She was exhausted. It was also getting late. She needed to call Barney Wilton in Summitville and postpone their meeting, then reschedule her doctor's appointment. After that, she needed to make a concrete plan of action. Fortunately she had just been paid for her work on the inn. It would give her the money to make another fresh start elsewhere.

The tears welled in her eyes and the pain stabbed at her heart. A fresh start... that was what she thought she was doing when she had left Laguna Beach and tried to put the horrible experience of Jerry Peterson behind her. She heaved a heavy sigh of despair, then reached for the phone.

Twelve

Darvi awoke with a start, the bath towel still wrapped around her body—only she was under the covers, with Rance sleeping beside her. It was still pouring rain.

She remembered stretching out on top of the bedspread, thinking she would rest for just a few moments, then get busy rescheduling her life. That was several hours ago. She had no memory of Rance's arrival, his covering her and lying down next to her. She gazed at his sleeping face, then tentatively reached over and carefully brushed some errant locks of hair from his forehead. She looked down at the dressing covering the stitches in his thigh. She wanted to cry as she delicately ran her fingers across the red marks on his cheek. She quietly slipped out of bed and dressed.

She sat on the edge of the bed, watching him. She had been torn about what to do. Should she wake him and tell him to go home and leave her alone? Or, knowing that he had not gotten any more sleep than she had the previous night, let him stay until he woke up on his own? Several hours passed before he stirred. He turned over, automatically reaching his arm out for her. As his weight twisted on his injured leg, he winced in pain and quickly sat up. It took him a couple of moments to get his bearings, to connect the previous night's events in his head. His fingers gently pushed at the bandage on his thigh, then ran across his scraped cheek and over his chin.

Darvi rose to her feet, determined to take immediate control of the situation. "Well, now that you're awake, you can get dressed and go back home. Give me back my front-door key. You're no longer welcome here." She tried to stop the tremors that passed through her body, one after the other. She hugged her arms around her shoulders in an effort to ward off the chill that slowly crept through her being. "You made it very clear that you don't want the baby and that you think I'm trying to trap you into something. Well, we certainly don't need you."

He reached out and grabbed her wrist, then pulled her down on the bed next to him. He twined his fingers in her long hair and nestled her head against his shoulder as he forced her into his embrace. "I'm sorry my words hurt you. I didn't mean for them to. It's just that you told me you couldn't have any children, then you turn up pregnant. I don't understand any of this pregnancy thing. I know we've never really discussed what direction we were going, what the future held, but..." His voice faltered, then he finally blurted out, "You're pushing me too much." His voice turned hard again. "I've been through this before... trapped into a marriage that was doomed from the start by a woman telling me she was pregnant.''

She had almost been lulled into a state of acceptance, a belief that he really had not meant what he had said. Then she heard the words and heard the resentment in his voice. She pulled free of his arms, her pain and anger hurtling through the air toward him. ''I'm pushing you? You've been pushing me from the day we meant, forcing me to talk about things I didn't want to face.'' She stormed across the room, putting some distance between them. ''And as for trying to tie you down with some ruse about being pregnant… well, only someone as arrogant as you would assume that every woman in the world considers you a prime catch!''

She glared at him as her tears overflowed her eyes and rolled down her cheeks. ''I never once said anything about marriage. Besides, I don't see why you're so upset. What makes you think you're even the father…'' She hesitated as a sob shuddered through her, then she thrust out her chin in defiance of him and his accusations. ''In fact, you're not the father. So there— you have no obligation to me or my baby. We'll get along just fine without any help from you.''

Her statement hit him like a splash of cold water in the face. What was he doing? He took a calming breath as he climbed out of bed, being careful of his bandaged leg. He crossed the room to where she stood. His eyes softened and his voice softened as he placed his trembling hands on her shoulders. She may have been putting up a brave front, but he could see how truly frightened she was—he could see it in the depths of her emerald eyes. At that very second he knew, beyond a shadow of a doubt, that the only thing more terrifying to him than making a lifetime commitment to Darvi was losing her forever.

He held her tightly as he studied her for a moment. "What do you think you're doing, giving me an out? Letting me off the hook? Of course I'm the father, it's my child." He drew her to him and held her tenderly in his arms.

He kissed her gently on the cheek as he whispered in her ear, "It's our child—a miracle created from our love." He rocked her in his arms. Then he continued, the love and caring he felt no longer hidden, "I love you, Darvi. I love you very much. You don't know how worried I've been about you, knowing that something was wrong but not knowing what. I've imagined every terrible thing that could be, but refused to accept any of them."

She was not sure she had heard him correctly. Could it be? Her voice was barely above a whisper. "Did...did you say love?"

"Yes, I did. I've wanted to tell you for a long time, as long ago as the first time we made love." He paused for a moment to gather the rest of his thoughts. "Just now, when I thought I had actually lost you—driven you away from me by giving vent to my own fears—I realized exactly how much I love you. I'm not afraid to say it anymore. I love you, Darvi. You're my entire life. Without you, I have nothing."

"You don't know how much I've longed to hear you say those words." She snuggled closer to him. "I love you with all my heart—in spite of all your faults." She raised her head and looked intently into his clear blue eyes. "Actually, other than being stubborn, arrogant, pushy and slightly possessive, you don't have too many faults."

He returned her look, his eyes crinkling with amusement and his voice taking on a teasing quality. "Oh, I see. Just those minor ones plus a few insignificant others." He brought his mouth to hers gently, filling her with his caring—with his unconditional love.

He continued to rock her in his arms as the enormity of the situation played through his mind. He closed his eyes and allowed a smile to curl the corners of his mouth. He kissed her on the forehead. "A baby. We're having a baby. I love you, Darvi Stanton. I love you so much. I can't believe this." He shook his head, not knowing what to say or how to behave. He led her over to the edge of the bed, where they sat down.

"Oh, Rance. I've been so scared the past few days. I didn't know what you'd think, how you'd take the news. Believe me, I was as surprised by all of this as you are. I didn't purposely mislead you—honest I didn't. I sincerely thought I couldn't get pregnant again. I thought I was coming down with the flu. I only went to the doctor so I'd be all right for the open house. And then when I finally worked up the nerve to tell you and you thought I was trying to manipulate you the way your ex-wife had..."

He continued to hold her, to stroke her hair. "We have things to talk about, plans to make. First of all—" he placed his fingertips beneath her chin and lifted her face so he could see into her eyes "—are you okay? Did the doctor say everything was all right?"

"Yes, everything is fine. I had a follow-up appointment for one o'clock today, but I rescheduled it as soon as I arrived home this morning. Now I go back Wednesday morning at nine."

"I'm going with you." He said it as a statement, not a question. He left her no room for argument or disagreement.

"Oh?" She looked at him with amusement. "You've decided that, have you?"

"Absolutely. That matter is settled. Now on to the next item. I think we should get married next week. We could be the inn's first honeymooners—"

"Married!" She blurted out the word, shocked by what he had just said. "If you think for one minute I want you to marry me simply because I'm pregnant, then you'd better think again. No way am I spending the rest of my life wondering if you married me because you wanted to or only because, once again, you felt trapped into doing the honorable thing."

His expression was serious as he plumbed the depths of her eyes. "No, I don't feel trapped. There are no more doubts or fears. I want very much for us to be married—it'll be next week."

He felt her tension melt away as she placed her head against his shoulder. "See what I mean? Stubborn, pushy and slightly possessive."

She raised her head, and he saw a flicker of anxiety dart through her eyes. Her expression became sober. She seemed to be searching his face for some sort of insight.

"Are you sure, Rance. Really sure?"

"Yes, I'm very sure. I've never been so sure of anything in my entire life." He sat quietly for a moment. "We'll be married. Our love has created a new life— we've produced a child. We'll be a family." He held her tightly, his words barely audible. "It's a miracle. It's more than I dared hope for, more than I dreamed could ever be. I'm so very happy."

He lowered his head to hers, his lips soft and tender as they met her mouth. Darvi felt his love as he kissed her. Her head was swimming, her mind in a complete muddle as the magnitude of what had happened overwhelmed her. Just the night before it seemed as if her entire world had come crashing down around her. And now she and Rance were going to be married—they were going to be a family. He was pleased about the baby, wanted the baby. Everything was so perfect, so wonderful.

She put her arms around his neck and returned his kiss, his love. Never in her life had she felt so full of love, joy and fulfillment as at that moment. Her emotions soared to the heavens. She felt as free to reach the emotional heights as was possible for any human being.

Darvi pulled her mouth away from his, her breathing ragged, matching his own. "Rance..."

He recaptured her mouth as his hand slowly slipped under her sweatshirt and unfastened her bra. He quickly and expertly removed her clothes as her hands slid across his bare chest, her fingers ruffled his chest hair.

He laid her back on the bed. Her head rested against the pillow as he gently cupped her exposed breast, reveling in the smoothness of her silky skin. As he slipped his tongue between her lips, he softly kneaded the firm flesh, teasing her nipple to a hard peak.

She eagerly responded to his touch, the sensual stirrings moving quickly through her body. Her tongue danced with his, her leg rubbed seductively against his leg, her hands caressed his back and shoulders.

Rance's lips moved across her cheek, down her neck to her shoulder. Tingling waves rippled across her skin. A moan of pleasure escaped her lips as he drew her nipple into his mouth, gently suckling, his tongue playing across the pebbled texture.

Darvi lost herself to his electrifying touch, to the heated passion building deep inside her. Never in her life had she believed love could be so marvelous, so full of pleasure, so steeped in the pure joy of living. She loved everything about Rance—the way he physically touched her body and the way he emotionally touched her soul.

He released her puckered nipple from his mouth, kissing the underside of her breast, before moving across her stomach. "Oh, Rance—I love you so much." She felt his fingertips trail across her abdomen, then run lightly up her inner thigh. She shuddered as a delicious sensation pulsed through her body.

Now his lips moved across her abdomen, titillating her skin. His fingertips lightly teased the folds of her femininity, heated her taut nerve endings.

They slowly and sensually shared the delights of their togetherness—their bodies and souls totally in sync, their unconditional love for each other filling the very air around them with an overwhelming joy.

Her copper hair fanned out to frame her glowing face. He nuzzled her neck as his heated passion slowly penetrated the moist warmth of her inner being. Darvi melded with his sensual rhythm, and they moved as one.

His voice was husky, breathless—his passions at such a pitch that speaking had become difficult. "I love you, Darvi. I love you so much, you and the baby."

The convulsions shook her body as his words released the incendiary sensations that had been rapidly building inside her. She felt him shudder as he tightened his hold on her, his own release quickly following hers.

The afternoon turned to evening as the rain continued to fall. They floated on an opalescent cloud, covered by a gossamer veil, as they savored every intimate moment of their togetherness.

Darvi slept in Rance's arms as he watched her face, listened to her slow, even breathing. He was still having difficulty comprehending the enormity of everything that had happened. He lightly touched his fingertips to her abdomen, marveling at the life they had created, the life growing in her womb. He leaned forward and gently kissed her abdomen, his lips touching the same place his fingers had just caressed. Then he rested his head against her stomach, wrapping his arms around her hips.

She slowly stirred and opened her eyes. She reached out her hand and brushed his cheek, her fingers touching the scrape marks on his face. She smiled as she saw the wonder on his face and the glow in his eyes. He raised his head, his mouth seeking out hers. He kissed her tenderly, then again rested his cheek against her stomach.

His voice was soft and loving, the strange mysteries of life filling his being. "Darvi, honey, did the doctor say whether it was going to be a boy or a girl?"

She chuckled as she ran her fingers through his tousled hair. "You're ahead of the game. The only tests that we did were to determine whether I was pregnant. The rest is yet to come."

He raised his head and looked at her. "Which do you want, a boy or a girl?"

She leaned forward and kissed him gently. "It doesn't make any difference. I'll be happy either way. How about you?"

For a moment, Rance looked pensive. "At first I wanted a little boy. I think that's natural. All men want a son to carry on the family name, to play ball with—" he grinned at her "—all that guy stuff." He became thoughtful again. "Then I started thinking about a little girl..." He brushed his fingertips across her cheek and tucked an errant tendril of hair behind her ear. "A precious little package who would look just like you. A beautiful little girl with emerald green eyes and copper-colored hair."

He sat up, drew her to him and held her tightly against him. "You know, Mrs. Coulter—Darvi Anne Coulter—I am the luckiest man on the face of the Earth."

She chuckled. "'Mrs. Coulter'? Isn't that just a bit premature?"

"Just trying it out to see if I like the way it sounds." He grinned at her. "It sounds good, it sounds right—it sounds perfect."

Epilogue

Darvi stood in the doorway of the workshop and watched as Rance sanded the wood to a satin smooth finish. She could see it in his face, in the way he paid meticulous attention to each and every detail, no matter how small, that the work was a labor of love.

The two-story dollhouse stood two and a half feet high, five feet wide and a foot and a half deep. He had started on it the day their daughter had been born— two weeks ago. Each and every room was built to scale and had all the details of a real house. There were closets with doors that actually opened and closed, shelves, cabinets and drawers that pulled out. There was a wide curving staircase between the floors, similar to the one at the inn. As soon as he finished the dollhouse he would start on the miniature furniture.

"You know she won't be old enough to play with it for quite a while." Darvi crossed from the door to the workbench, carrying the tiny pink bundle in her arms.

Rance looked up at the sound of her voice, surprised to see her standing there. He had been so absorbed in his work he had not heard her enter the room. He put his tools down, wiped the sawdust from his hands and arms and smiled at his family. His face radiated his pleasure at seeing them. He brushed a loving kiss against Darvi's lips, then gently touched his fingertip to his daughter's cheek. "Darvi, honey, isn't it time for Jillian to be in bed?"

"I was just about to tuck her in. I thought I'd give you a chance to say good-night."

He glanced at his watch. "I think I'll call it a night out here. Give me a moment and I'll go with you." He cleaned up his work area, then they went into the house.

"Here, let me." Rance took the baby from Darvi and held her in his arms, wonder in his eyes as he peered at her tiny face. His words came out as almost a whisper. "She's beautiful, just like you." He carefully placed his daughter in the crib—the crib he had made by hand. "Good night, little Jillian. I love you."

Rance clasped Darvi's hand in his as they left the nursery. They walked down the hallway together to the living room and settled onto the couch. The flames danced in the fireplace, throwing soft patterns of light and shadow across the walls. He put his arm around her shoulder and drew her against him. "I love you, Mrs. Coulter." He leaned over and placed a soft kiss on her lips. "I love you very much."

''I love you, too, Mr. Coulter.''

They sat in silence, basking in the golden glow of their love.

*   *   *   *   *

Get Ready to be Swept Away by
Silhouette's Spring Collection

Abduction *&* Seduction

These passion-filled stories explore both the dangerous
desires of men and the seductive powers of women.
Written by three of our most celebrated authors, they are
sure to capture your hearts.

Diana Palmer
Brings us a spin-off of her Long, Tall Texans series

Joan Johnston
Crafts a beguiling Western romance

Rebecca Brandewyne
New York Times bestselling author
makes a smashing contemporary debut

Available in March at your favorite retail outlet.

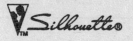

Take 4 bestselling love stories FREE

Plus get a FREE surprise gift!

Special Limited-time Offer

Mail to Silhouette Reader Service™

3010 Walden Avenue
P.O. Box 1867
Buffalo, N.Y. 14269-1867

YES! Please send me 4 free Silhouette Desire® novels and my free surprise gift. Then send me 6 brand-new novels every month, which I will receive months before they appear in bookstores. Bill me at the low price of $2.44 each plus 25¢ delivery and applicable sales tax, if any.* That's the complete price and—compared to the cover prices of $2.99 each—quite a bargain! I understand that accepting the books and gift places me under no obligation ever to buy any books. I can always return a shipment and cancel at any time. Even if I never buy another book from Silhouette, the 4 free books and the surprise gift are mine to keep forever.

225 BPA ANRS

Name	(PLEASE PRINT)	
Address	Apt. No.	
City	State	Zip

This offer is limited to one order per household and not valid to present Silhouette Desire® subscribers. *Terms and prices are subject to change without notice.
Sales tax applicable in N.Y.

UDES-94R   ©1990 Harlequin Enterprises Limited

MONTANA
Mavericks

Stories that capture living and loving
beneath the Big Sky, where legends live
on...and mystery lingers.

This January, the intrigue continues with

OUTLAW LOVERS
by Pat Warren

He was a wanted man. She was the beckoning angel
who offered him a hideout. Now their budding
passion has put them both in danger. And he'd do
anything to protect her.

Don't miss a minute of the loving as the passion
continues with:

WAY OF THE WOLF
by Rebecca Daniels (February)

THE LAW IS NO LADY
by Helen R. Myers (March)

FATHER FOUND
by Laurie Paige (April)
and many more!

Only from ▼ *Silhouette*® where passion lives.

The Loop™

Is the future what it's cracked up to be?

This January, get outta town with Marissa in

GETTING A LIFE: MARISSA
by Kathryn Jensen

Marissa was speeding down the fast lane, heading nowhere fast. Her life was a series of hot parties, hot dates...and getting herself out of hot water. Until, one day, she realized that she had nowhere to go but... home. Returning to her hick town wasn't exactly her idea of a good time, but it was better than dodging phone calls from collection agencies and creepy guys. So Marissa packed up her bags, got on the bus—and discovered that her troubles had just begun!

The ups and downs of life as you know it continue with

GETTING OUT: EMILY
by ArLynn Presser (February)

GETTING AWAY WITH IT: JOJO
by Liz Ireland (March)

Get smart. Get into "The Loop"!

Only from **∇ Silhouette®**
TM

where passion lives.

SILHOUETTE®

Desire

MAN of the MONTH
1995

Don't let the winter months get you down because the heat is about to get turned way up...with the sexiest hunks of 1995!

January: *A NUISANCE*
by Lass Small

February: *COWBOYS DON'T CRY*
by Anne McAllister

March: *THAT BURKE MAN*
the 75th Man of the Month
by Diana Palmer

April: *MR. EASY*
by Cait London

May: *MYSTERIOUS MOUNTAIN MAN*
by Annette Broadrick

June: *SINGLE DAD*
by Jennifer Greene

**MAN OF THE MONTH...
ONLY FROM
SIILHOUETTE DESIRE**

Robert...Luke...Noah
Three proud, strong brothers who live—and love—by

THE CODE OF THE WEST

Meet the Tanner man, starting with Silhouette Desire's *Man of the Month* for February, Robert Tanner, in Anne McAllister's

COWBOYS DON'T CRY

Robert Tanner never let any woman get close to him—especially not Maggie MacLeod. But the tempting new owner of his ranch was determined to get past the well-built defenses around his heart....

And be sure to watch for brothers Luke and Noah, in their own stories, COWBOYS DON'T QUIT and COWBOYS DON'T STAY, throughout 1995!

Only from

SILHOUETTE... Where Passion Lives

Don't miss these Silhouette favorites by some of our most
distinguished authors! And now you can receive a discount by
ordering two or more titles!

SD#05786	QUICKSAND by Jennifer Greene	$2.89	☐
SD#05795	DEREK by Leslie Guccione	$2.99	☐
SD#05818	NOT JUST ANOTHER PERFECT WIFE		
	by Robin Elliott	$2.99	☐
IM#07505	HELL ON WHEELS by Naomi Horton	$3.50	☐
IM#07514	FIRE ON THE MOUNTAIN		
	by Marion Smith Collins	$3.50	☐
IM#07559	KEEPER by Patricia Gardner Evans	$3.50	☐
SSE#09879	LOVING AND GIVING by Gina Ferris	$3.50	☐
SSE#09892	BABY IN THE MIDDLE	$3.50 U.S.	☐
	by Marie Ferrarella	$3.99 CAN.	☐
SSE#09902	SEDUCED BY INNOCENCE	$3.50 U.S.	☐
	by Lucy Gordon	$3.99 CAN.	☐
SR#08952	INSTANT FATHER by Lucy Gordon	$2.75	☐
SR#08984	AUNT CONNIE'S WEDDING		
	by Marie Ferrarella	$2.75	☐
SR#08990	JILTED by Joleen Daniels	$2.75	☐

(limited quantities available on certain titles)

AMOUNT	$_____
DEDUCT: 10% DISCOUNT FOR 2+ BOOKS	$_____
POSTAGE & HANDLING	$_____
($1.00 for one book, 50¢ for each additional)	
APPLICABLE TAXES*	$_____
TOTAL PAYABLE	$_____
(check or money order—please do not send cash)	

To order, complete this form and send it, along with a check or money order
for the total above, payable to Silhouette Books, to: **in the U.S.:** 3010 Walden
Avenue, P.O. Box 9077, Buffalo, NY 14269-9077; **in Canada:** P.O. Box 636,
Fort Erie, Ontario, L2A 5X3.

Name:_____

Address:_____City:_____

State/Prov.:_____Zip/Postal Code:_____

*New York residents remit applicable sales taxes.
Canadian residents remit applicable GST and provincial taxes.   SBACK-DF

V *Silhouette*®
TM